W9-CHO-150

Faith is playing matchmaker and Liza may get burned!

Winnie's lost in a blizzard—and this time her friends can't save her.

KC's in love— with a guy who's after more than her heart!

KC sipped her hot cocoa

as she, Faith, Liza, and Winnie listened to Kimberly and Casper's astonishing tale of their encounter with Jake Tower. With every word Kimberly spoke, she could feel herself becoming more and more outraged. "That family is out of control," she said when Kimberly was done. "You guys could have been seriously hurt. Where is this going to end?"

"Do you think he would destroy the whole ski season just to get at your mom?" Faith asked, stoking the fire in the stone fireplace. "That's so outrageous that it's unbelievable. If it's true it's scary."

"No kidding, it's scary," Casper agreed. "The Towers are a family of psychos, if you ask me."

Don't miss these books
in the exciting FRESHMAN DORM series

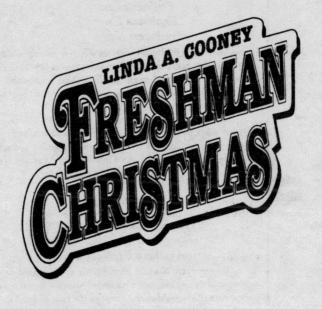

LINDA A. COONEY

FRESHMAN CHRISTMAS

HarperPaperbacks
A Division of HarperCollins*Publishers*

This is a work of fiction. The characters, incidents, and dialogues are products of the author's imagination and are not to be construed as real. Any resemblance to actual events or persons, living or dead, is entirely coincidental.

HarperPaperbacks   *A Division of* HarperCollins*Publishers*
10 East 53rd Street, New York, N.Y. 10022

Cover illustration by Tony Greco

First printing: December 1992

Printed in the United States of America

HarperPaperbacks and colophon are trademarks of HarperCollins*Publishers*

❖ 10 9 8 7 6 5 4 3 2 1

One

"**W**ow!" gasped KC Angeletti, sitting forward in the front seat of Kimberly Dayton's van. The most spectacular mountain range KC had ever seen—jagged, snow-covered peaks etched against a vast ice-blue sky—had just come into view.

Winnie Gottlieb leaned forward from the backseat. Her papier-mâché banana earrings dangled softly. "Is the whole state of Montana like a giant movie set or what?" she asked. "I mean, it's awesome here."

In the seat beside Winnie, Faith Crowley opened her eyes and plumped the pillow she had nestled between her head and the window. "I feel like we've been driving through a western movie for the last two hours," she said. "I've even been dreaming of cowboys."

"Okay, psych major," KC said to Winnie. "What does *that* mean?"

Winnie sat up straight and pointed one finger in the air. "Ze dream of ze old cowboys," she began in a heavy mock-German accent. "Is clearly an indication zat ze patient ate one too many tacos at ze last Taco Bell stop."

"Thank you for that brilliant analysis, professor." Faith laughed before pulling her University of Springfield sweatshirt all the way up over her blond hair and turning her face back into her pillow.

A loud snap of gum made KC look over to Liza Ruff, who was stretched out on the long backseat of the van, blowing large pink bubbles of gum. "I'd like to meet a dreamy cowboy on this trip," Liza said, twirling a fake lasso over her head. "As soon as I see one, I'm going to rope him right in. I'll catch one for each of you—except Winnie. Married gals tend to the homestead. But the rest of us need a little cowboy action. Let me at 'em!" Liza stuck out her ample chest and let loose with her version of a cowboy cry. "Ya-hoooooo! Yippee-i-ki-aaaaa."

Faith peeked out from under her shirt and rolled her eyes. KC smiled at her. She knew Faith felt bad about inviting her roommate Liza along. Although none of them was exactly thrilled with Liza—she was so brash and loud, with her tight neon clothing and carrot-red curls—KC was glad Liza had come. In fact, she was grateful to all of them for coming, especially since it meant spending the holidays away from home.

They had left Springfield, Oregon, for Montana to help KC's mother get the Angel Dude Ranch ready and running in time for the ski season. Mrs. Angeletti had moved there since the death of her husband.

KC looked at Faith's long blond braid peeking out from under the heather-gray sweatshirt. They'd picked up Faith right outside the theater-department building, because she was delivering the last of her final projects at the latest possible moment. She'd been up the whole night before, finishing a set design for her Introduction to Technical Theater course. From there, she'd jumped into Kimberly's van and made the long trip, trying desperately to catch up on sleep along the way.

In her heart, KC had known she could count on Faith. But she was pleasantly surprised that Winnie had volunteered to come. Even though she, Faith, and Winnie had been best friends all through high school, she and Winnie had grown apart in college. It just seemed to KC that the personality differences between them had become more pronounced. She found herself being short-tempered with flaky Winnie. Still, she loved her old friend and hoped Winnie's recent marriage to Josh Gaffey might make her less scatty.

She looked at Winnie, who was now slouched down in the seat reading a copy of *Mad* magazine. Winnie was so buried in the magazine that her Micky-Mouse-print leggings, red high-top shoes with their lace bows, and bright-red tunic top were all KC could see. At least Winnie was a true original.

"Want me to drive for a while?" KC asked Kimberly.

"Thanks, but I'm okay," Kimberly replied.

For a quick moment, KC studied Kimberly's smooth dark skin and delicate profile. She was glad she'd have the chance to get to know her better on this trip. From the first time KC had met Faith's dorm neighbor, she'd admired her effortless grace and easy sophistication.

As if sensing KC observing her, Kimberly gave her a sidelong glance. "We're almost there," she said. "Excited?"

"Sure am," KC answered. "I've always heard about this ranch from my Grandma Rose, but I've never come out here. I still can't believe she just *gave* it to my mom."

"That *was* pretty generous of her," Kimberly agreed.

"She must have figured Mom needed something to focus on, now that my father's gone." KC heard her own voice catch at the mention of her father. His recent death still didn't seem real to her. She couldn't accept that she'd never see him again. She knew her mother felt the same way.

"Sometimes a total change can be good for a person," Kimberly observed.

"This is certainly a total change," said KC, smiling. "I hope she can make the ranch work as a vacation spot. Even though the place was a gift, she's had to sink all her money into renovating it. She sold The Windchime, our health-food restaurant in Oregon, and invested all her savings into this place. If it doesn't work out, I don't know what she'll do."

"That's why *we're* here," said Winnie, popping her head up from behind the magazine and fussing with her short, spiky, brown hair in the rearview mirror. "To make sure your mom is ready for the mad Christmas rush, which is going to make her rich, rich, rich!"

"I can't thank you guys enough," KC said. "I know you'd all rather be home for the holidays."

"No problem," said Faith. "My mother was a little sad at first, but she got over it."

"My parents were thrilled," Liza said. She laughed scornfully. "They got to go to Florida without having to cough up the money for a plane ticket for *moi*."

"You missed going to Florida?" KC said regretfully. "I didn't know."

"No problem. Really," Liza assured her. "Being stuffed into an over-air-conditioned condo with my parents and their ancient friends is not my idea of fun."

"Christmas at my house can be dull, too," Kimberly said. "Besides, Christmas break is pretty long. We have practically the whole month of January off."

"I need a long break after last semester," KC said. She'd worked hard to keep up the grades required by her sorority, the Tri Betas. It hadn't been easy. KC was truly shocked by how much harder the schoolwork was at the University of Springfield, compared to high school.

"Hey, civilization at last!" Kimberly cried as they drove into a small downtown area.

"I wouldn't exactly call this civilization," Winnie scoffed, looking over the wide main street lined by brick two-story buildings on either side.

KC suddenly felt a pang of hunger. "Anybody for lunch?"

"Yeah. I'm famished," said Kimberly. "Feed me a juicy hamburger."

"Well, don't get your hopes up," Winnie said. "I don't see a single golden arch."

"Thank goodness," sighed KC. After two days on the road, she'd had her fill of fast food. On the right, a building with an interesting sign caught her eye. It was painted with a picture of a black stallion leaping over a brilliant yellow sun against a red background. Above the stallion were the words "The Hungry Horse." The sign jutted out, hanging on an iron pole. "How about that place?" she suggested.

"It looks good to me," Kimberly said as she pulled to the curb.

"Where are we, anyway?" Faith asked, putting her feet into her trademark cowboy boots.

Kimberly picked up the carelessly folded map on the dashboard. "Towerton," she replied.

"Then we're here," KC said. "Mom's ranch is about three miles past downtown Towertown. Maybe we should just keep going."

"Sorry, but nature is calling," Liza spoke up. "I need a pit stop."

"Me, too," said Winnie.

As they trooped down the street, KC took in the odd mix of old and new shops. It was as if there were two Towertons. One was a real no-frills western town with a feed-and-grain store, a hardware store, and a used car lot filled mostly with secondhand jeeps and pickup trucks. The other Towerton was obviously there to accommodate and impress the tourists who came to ski. Renée's Scent Boutique, a duplex movie theater, the Indian Works craft and art gallery—they all seemed a little out of place on this plain strip of brick buildings.

"Do you think this is a real cowboy hangout?" Liza asked excitedly outside the heavy wooden front door of The Hungry Horse with its large Christmas wreath.

"We'll soon find out," Faith said, pushing the door.

As soon as she stepped into the dark hallway, KC inhaled the sweetness of beer and the woodsy smell of sawdust-covered floors. Farther inside KC observed that the restaurant was split into two parts: In the front was a long, dark bar. Three broad-shouldered men, all in plaid flannel shirts and jeans, hunkered over their beers.

A waitress with a frilly apron over her jeans and big, moussed hair approached them. "Table for five," Liza told her imperiously, making KC want to slip to the back of the group in embarrassment.

"This way, ladies," the waitress said with a western twang. She seated them in the empty back room, where simple wooden tables and chairs bordered a rectangular dance floor.

"This is so cool!" Liza cried as they surveyed their menus. "Someday when I'm a big star, I'm going to make a movie here. There'll be a part for every one of you. KC, you can be the haughty beauty from the snooty family. Winnie, you can be the bar floozy. Kimberly can be one of the can can girl-type-dancers. And Faith, you can be the sweet rancher's daughter, or else you can direct it."

"Who will you be?" asked Faith.

"The star. I'll be the madam with the heart of gold who runs the local brothel. You all hate me at first, but then I save the day and you all have to admit you were wrong. My name will be Belle Starr or something like that."

"I don't want to be the bar floozy," Winnie objected. "How about if I'm the progressive schoolteacher who believes in Darwinism, which nobody understands yet?"

Liza shrugged. "If you like." She got up from the table. "But I must use the john. Order me a hamburger and fries."

"Wait for me," said Winnie, joining Liza as she left in search of the bathroom.

"Am I haughty?" KC asked, stung by Liza's words.

"Don't listen to her. Liza's insane," Faith told Kimberly and KC. "I'm sorry to inflict her on you, but she made it so obvious that she was dying to come that I just had to invite her."

"She's not that bad," Kimberly said. "I actually think she does have a heart of gold."

"Maybe. Anyway, she's another pair of hands," KC said, resigned to put up with Liza. While Faith and Kimberly studied their menus, KC's gray eyes roamed restlessly around the room. Rodeo trophies were perched on high shelves, and black-and-white photos of rodeo riders were the only other wall adornments besides a string of colorful, twinkling Christmas lights. The Hungry Horse sure seemed to be the real thing, a genuine western hang out, not some dressed-up tourist trap. KC looked down at her paper napkin and saw the words "The Hungry Horse, feeding folks since 1910!"

It was odd to think that Grandma Rose might have come to this place as a young woman. KC recalled what her mother had told her about why Grandma Rose left Montana. She'd been engaged to a rich cattle baron, her neighbor Lewiston

Tower. But then Rose had fallen in love with Antony Angeletti, a businessman her father knew. Grandma Rose had had a hard time breaking it off with Lewiston. He hadn't been a man to take rejection easily. Apparently he had become enraged and made life unpleasant for Rose. When she left town, he swore he'd never let go of the fury in his heart.

"What are you thinking?" Faith asked.

"I'm remembering a story about my grandmother and a guy she used to be engaged to," KC told her. "His name was Lewiston Tower, and he lived at the neighboring ranch."

"Tower, huh? Is this town named after his family?" asked Kimberly.

KC nodded. "They were a real powerful family from way, way back. My grandmother would have been super-rich if she'd married him."

"Oh, you mean instead of being just very rich now?" Faith said, laughing.

"Okay, okay. It's true Rose did all right," KC admitted. "But at the time, my grandfather didn't have a lot of money, and the Tower family was loaded."

"She gave up riches for love. That's awfully romantic," Kimberly muttered dreamily.

"What's romantic?" Liza asked as she and Winnie returned.

"KC's grandmother left a wealthy cattle baron for a poor man she loved," Faith filled her in.

Liza raised one skeptical eyebrow. "I wouldn't mind being hooked up with a cattle baron."

The waitress came and took their orders. "I'm going to call Mom," KC said when the waitress was gone.

She found a public phone in a narrow dark hallway off the bar. After putting a quarter in the slot, she punched in the number of the ranch. The phone rang . . . and rang . . . and rang. "Not exactly the best way to do business," KC mumbled.

While she hung on the ringing line, KC looked at a local-events bulletin board by the phone. Her eyes wandered past the notices for a church supper and a winter carnival.

Suddenly, her breath caught sharply in her throat.

In the middle of the board was a poster featuring a black-and-white photo of a dark-haired young man riding a bucking bronco. The horse was arched at a dangerous angle, but the guy held on with one hand. His cowboy hat was clutched in his free hand, which he waved above his head. He was handsome, graceful, and wild. A shot of sharp sunlight bounced off his chin and high cheekbones. There was a look of animal determination in his eyes.

KC stared at his face, trying to extricate more detail than the slightly blurred photo was willing to surrender. Something about him stopped her cold.

Above the photo was an announcement for an indoor holiday rodeo. It would be held right in Towerton. KC's heart skipped a beat. The rider was sure to be there.

"Hello?" Mrs. Angeletti finally came on the line. "Is anyone there? Hello?"

"Mom!" KC snapped back to reality. "What if I was trying to make a reservation? I would have hung up long ago!"

"Sorry, hon. I was out in the stables."

"Don't you have anyone there to answer the phone?"

"I will as soon as you get here," her mother said happily. "Where are you?"

"In Towerton."

"You're just ten minutes away."

"I know. We're eating something quick, then we'll be right over. It sounds like you need help."

"Don't remind me." Mrs. Angeletti laughed grimly. "I'm dying to see you."

"Me, too. We'll be there soon." Gently, KC replaced the phone receiver and stared once more at the photo. The cowboy's image mesmerized her all over again. What was he feeling up there on that bucking horse? He looked as if he could ride the horse on the sign out front, and leap over the sun, too.

A tap on her shoulder made KC jump. "Everything okay?" Faith asked, coming up beside her. "You looked like you were in a trance. What's so interesting on that board?"

"I was just reading about this rodeo," KC said, pointing to the photo. "And admiring the rider."

Faith smiled. "Hunky guy. But your burger arrived, and it's getting cold."

KC found it strange that Faith could look at the photo and remain so casual. Somehow, though, she didn't want to discuss it. Her connection with the cowboy seemed too personal to talk about.

The two girls walked back to the table and found Liza, Kimberly, and Winnie huddled together over a newspaper.

"This is the local paper," Winnie told them. "The waitress gave it to us to look through. There's going to be a real rodeo soon."

"Let me see," said KC, hoping there was another photo of the rodeo rider. Instead, she looked over Liza's shoulder and saw a picture of a slender blond man dressed in a long barn jacket and a cowboy hat.

"The article says he's one of the Tower twins, Jake Tower," Liza said. "His family holds a big Christmas barn dance. That's what the newspaper story is about."

"A dance, huh?" Winnie sighed. "If we go, I won't be able to dance."

"Why not?" Faith asked.

"I'm a married woman now," Winnie reminded her. "I can't go dancing with strange guys. I wish Josh had come."

"How come you didn't go with him to see his new niece in California?" Kimberly asked.

Winnie shrugged and sipped her soda. "I figured it was more important to help out Mrs. Angeletti. I mean, in high school I spent so much time at her house, I feel like she's my second mother. I used to have Chanukkah at my house and Christmas with the Angelettis."

That memory caused a small knot in KC's stomach. This would be the first Christmas since her father's death. Not only that, but her brothers wouldn't be there, either. They'd opened up a restaurant together and couldn't get away to come to the ranch. Actually, KC was secretly glad they wouldn't be there. It would make her father's absence less conspicuous.

They ate quickly and paid. "You gals should

come back for some dancing," the waitress said as she put their change on the table. "We get real foot-stompin' bands here."

"Oh, we definitely will," Liza assured her.

Once they were back in the van, it took only minutes to leave downtown Towerton. In another five minutes, they turned off the paved road and were soon bouncing along on a dirt road. Above them, huge gray clouds billowed ominously and a light rain began to fall. "I'm glad we're almost there," said Kimberly. "I hate driving through storms, and it looks like one is coming."

As she had predicted, rain mixed with sleet soon began to cover the windshield. Kimberly flipped on the wipers and hunched forward to see better.

"Did you hear that?" Winnie asked.

KC nodded. Off in the distance she had heard an animal howl. "I guess we're in coyote country," she said. They drove on, passing miles and miles of fenced-in rangeland. "The Tower Ranch," KC read a sign along the way.

Finally they came to a small sign marked Lawder Lane. Lawder had been Grandma Rose's maiden name. "Turn here," KC instructed Kimberly.

After a short drive they came to a wooden fence. Behind it was a two-story log lodge with a wide front porch and a big wagon wheel in the front yard. A bright yellow and brown sign beside the wheel read "Angel Dude Ranch."

"It's great," said Faith.

"It sure is, and—" KC cut herself short. To the right of the lodge was a horse corral, and four horses were in the process of running wildly toward the gate.

The next thing she saw were two horsemen in long coats and cowboy hats, riding around the corral. Both had blond ponytails and slight frames. Their coats and hats obscured any other details, but KC knew her mother hadn't hired any stablehands yet. Something wasn't right.

"Stop, Kimberly," she cried. Kimberly put on the brakes. KC was out the door in a second, just in time to see one of the riders throw open the corral gate, urging the horses to race away.

"Hey!" KC shouted angrily as she jumped up onto the fence. "Hey!"

One of the riders turned and spotted her. He rode his horse straight over. KC recognized him right away. He was Jake Tower—or maybe he was the twin brother. He looked just the same as he had in his newspaper picture. The other blond rider was obviously his twin.

"What are you doing?" KC yelled at him. "You have no right to be here."

"Consider this a friendly warning," he snarled, his blue eyes narrowing menacingly. "Next time—"

"A warning about what?" KC demanded.

"Go back where you came from," he replied, spitting out the words. With that, he turned and galloped off toward his partner.

KC wiped the cold wetness from her forehead and watched the Tower twins disappear into the driving rain.

Two

Kimberly brushed aside a pine branch, which snapped back and sprayed her with icy water. She shivered with annoyance. There was nothing she hated more than this kind of wet cold. It got right into her skin and was making its way into her bones. She and Faith had been slogging through the icy, wet woods for nearly an hour. "Why did we volunteer to do this?" she asked.

"Because we know horses. Remember?" Faith replied.

"Oh, right. We're the hotshot horsewomen who are going to find the runaway hoofed beasts.

Do you think we promised the impossible?"

Faith smiled at her as they kept moving through a gently sloping patch of dense pines. "Nah. They've got to be around. They're not wild horses. They wouldn't just keep running."

So far, this wasn't turning out to be the light-hearted, carefree vacation Kimberly had hoped for. When Faith had told her KC needed help out on the ranch, Kimberly had leapt at the chance. She'd always longed to see the rugged West. Something in the pictures she'd seen had captivated her. The brilliant expanse of sky and imperious mountains seemed to speak of a wild freedom she wanted to experience. Besides that, she just needed to have some fun. The last semester had been grueling and full of tensions. There had been pressure when she'd dropped out of the extremely competitive dance department. There had been academic pressure and romantic disappointments. She'd even experienced some racial tension after a rumor had spread that she was stealing money in her dorm. So on this vacation she planned to kick back and have a good time.

But so far, it hadn't been so great. For starters, only KC and she could drive a stick shift, so all the driving had fallen to them. Kimberly's neck was stiff, and she had an annoying crimp in her right knee. She'd never driven for so many miles, and she didn't look forward to the trip back.

And now this. When she'd wanted nothing more than to get out of the van and collapse, this had to happen. But she had to do something. KC was so upset and didn't know what to tell her mother. Winnie and Liza certainly couldn't have handled it. Winnie probably would have gotten hopelessly lost, and Liza would have scared the horses off with her loud mouth, bright hair, and neon clothing. Thank goodness at least sensible, capable Faith was there to help too.

Kimberly kicked her way through a patch of prickly underbrush. A spindly branch caught on her shiny, loden-green rain boots, and as she bent to detach it, she caught sight of something moving in the clearing several yards away. "Look," she said, pointing. Up ahead a white and brown mare was grazing near a stream.

A twig cracked under Kimberly's boot, and the horse looked up sharply, on the alert for danger.

"Time to test our oat-shaking plan," Faith said.

Kimberly nodded and the two advanced cautiously toward the horse, holding out a paper bag filled with oats. "Hey, girl. Hi, girl," Kimberly cooed, rustling the oats as she spoke. "Want to eat something good?"

The horse stood stock-still, eyeing Kimberly

intently. "Don't you want to go home?" Kimberly continued gently. "Sure you do."

With a soft whinny, the mare nuzzled into the bag and began eating the offered oats. "Good girl," Kimberly soothed, running her hand down the horse's smooth neck. "Good girl." She turned to Faith. "Can you rope her?"

Faith nodded, deftly tying one end of rope over the horse's neck. "Why would those guys do such a mean and unreasonable thing?" Faith questioned as she worked.

"Welcome to the wonderful world of hate and prejudice." Kimberly laughed sadly.

Faith shot her a confused glance. "What do you mean?"

"It's like what happened to me in the dorm," Kimberly explained. "Remember when I was accused of stealing? I've never stolen a thing in my life, not even a ballpoint pen, but everyone assumed I did it, because I'm black."

"I remember. That was horrible. But I don't get the connection."

"It's the same for Mrs. Angeletti. She's an outsider, so the people around here are bound to mistrust her. People make assumptions about other people without bothering to find out who they are or what they're about."

"I wonder if that's it," Faith said, patting the

horse. "Doesn't it seem like more than a coincidence that the Tower twins did this? I mean, after what happened with KC's grandmother and their grandfather and all?"

"That was a long time ago," Kimberly pointed out. "I doubt they're getting vengeance for their grandfather."

"It does seem a bit farfetched," Faith admitted. "But maybe their grandfather ordered them to do it."

"Maybe," Kimberly said. "Anything is possible, I suppose. It just seems like an awfully long time to hold that kind of grudge."

With Faith holding the rope, they continued through the woods, looking for the other three horses. "I hope this doesn't upset Mrs. Angeletti too much," Kimberly said.

"If I know KC, she won't even tell her mom until we've got the horses back," Faith answered.

It wasn't long before they came upon the second horse, a gray mare drinking from a thin brook that rushed along in a series of small cascading waterfalls. When they approached, the mare looked up. She seemed unconcerned.

"Can you ride bareback?" Faith asked as she efficiently roped the docile horse.

"I've never done it," said Kimberly.

"Me neither," Faith admitted. "Want to try?"

Kimberly laughed nervously. "Not really. But I guess it'd be a lot faster on horseback."

Faith roped the gray horse, then struggled to pull herself up onto her back. "Let me tell you, it's a lot easier with stirrups," she said once she'd straightened up.

Kimberly led her horse beside a boulder. "Nature's step stool," she joked as she easily mounted the horse from the rock. "Let's go." Kimberly clutched the horse's coarse mane as they trotted along. With her thighs, she gripped the horse's sides and hoped she'd be able to figure out how to steer the animal without the help of reins when the time came to turn.

She looked over at Faith and noticed how fluidly her friend rode, despite the lack of saddle. Kimberly knew Faith had been a counselor at a drama camp last summer and she'd probably ridden a lot there. But it was more than that. With her lean, athletic figure and natural, pretty face, Faith looked as if she was born to be a cowgirl. Liza had been right about one thing. Faith *could* play the rancher's sweet daughter in a movie.

As she observed her, Kimberly suddenly realized that Faith was laughing softly to herself. "What's so funny?" she asked.

"I just got a funny image in my head. I was picturing Liza trying to ride bareback."

"Oh, God." Kimberly laughed. "I can just see her bouncing along, sliding from side to side, swearing at the horse at the top of her lungs."

"That's kind of the picture I got, too," Faith said with a smile. "I know she's got a good heart, but she drives me crazy. Two days stuck in a van with her is my idea of hell. It's like she's always up in your face. And the way she dresses! I get embarrassed to be seen with her."

"I guess she's not the prize roommate," Kimberly sympathized. "It must get hard for you."

"Tell me about it," said Faith. "At least it's not the total disaster it was in the beginning. She does kind of grow on you. I just wish she wasn't such a busybody—always butting in and eavesdropping. That's how she found out about this trip. She overheard me talking to KC on the phone. I didn't even know she was there, because she stood just outside the door until I was done talking. She deliberately eavesdropped, just because she *had* to know what I was saying. It makes me want to scream."

"Do you tell her how you feel?"

"Of course. But it's like she doesn't care. That's how I know she'll make it in show business. Rejection will just bounce right off her. She'll keep barreling on, no matter what anyone else says or does."

Kimberly laughed. "That's one of the things I like about her. She doesn't get insulted over little stuff, and she tries very hard to be agreeable."

"Too hard," Faith commented. "And she's always pushing me when it comes to guys. You'd think she was some kind of love authority, and yet she's never had a steady boyfriend. I hope she doesn't play matchmaker for me on this trip. Guys are the last thing I want to think about. I'm burned out on the opposite sex."

Kimberly had seen the effect Faith had on guys. She wasn't the drop-dead beauty KC was, but she was pretty and lively. She'd jump into a campus game of touch football and come out with three invitations to go out on the weekend.

"Does your burnout include Alec Brady?" Kimberly asked. She couldn't imagine burning out on a relationship with a famous movie star like Alec. Faith had met him when she worked on the crew of a science-fiction movie called *U and Me*, being shot at the University of Springfield.

Faith was getting ahead of Kimberly. Shifting her body weight, she pulled her horse around in a small circle and waited. "Alec was a dream," Faith admitted a little sadly when Kimberly's horse was head-to-head with her own. "But I haven't heard from him since filming finished."

"Why don't you call him?" Kimberly suggested.

"You parted friends and he gave you his private, unlisted number."

"Yeah, but I don't want to seem like a . . . a groupie. I have self-respect. He has *my* number. He can call me."

"I guess so," Kimberly agreed. "I get carried away with a person's image sometimes. That's what happened with Derek Weldon. He was so good-looking and funny that it took me a long time to see he was a real macho jerk."

"Alec wasn't a jerk," Faith said. "He was really nice." They began riding again, side by side, until they came out of the woods into a clearing. Acres and acres of short, wet grass rolled before them, occasionally marked off by low wooden-rail fences. Above them, fat storm clouds hovered threateningly in a vast, gray sky. Thick fog hung just above the ground. Peering through it, Kimberly saw no sign of the remaining two horses.

They rode on in silence, skirting the wooded area to their left. Kimberly hoped the horses hadn't gone into these woods. She hated the thought of going back in and being slapped with cold, wet pines all over again. Then, around a bend in the trees, she spotted the two remaining horses grazing just outside the border of the forest.

The first one Faith roped easily. The second

one, a black horse with a white marking on his forehead, was more skittish. He neighed and ran a short way off.

"Time for the oat offering," Kimberly sighed as she slid down off her horse. Holding her horse's rope in one hand and the oat bag in the other, she walked slowly forward. The loose horse neighed again and backed away. Kimberly rattled the bag. "Toasty oats. Come and get 'em."

Shifting on his legs, the horse seemed undecided, but he let Kimberly get close enough to wave the oats under his nose. After a little more coaxing, Kimberly got him to eat.

As she stood there holding the bag, she heard a sound coming from a stand of trees that jutted out from the forest. She turned quickly and saw the outline of a male figure staggering clumsily through the brush.

"Faith," she called sharply in a loud whisper. Faith rode over to her, leading the other horse. Kimberly jerked her head toward the trees. "We have company."

Faith tensed. "Is it the Tower twins?" she asked softly. The shadowy figure was moving slowly toward them. With darting eyes, Kimberly looked into the misty trees, trying to catch sight of a second Tower twin. She didn't want to be taken by surprise. Her muscles tightened and her heart pounded as a charge of adrenaline coursed through her.

When sensing danger, animals prepare for flight or fight. She remembered those words from her Psych 101 course. She didn't relish the idea of fighting, but she *did* want to prepare for flight.

"Faith, can you get down and help me tie up this horse?" Kimberly whispered, not taking her eyes off the figure moving through the trees. "We should be prepared to split *mucho* fast."

Faith lowered herself from her horse and began tying up the black horse as he fed from the oat bag. Kimberly kept her eyes glued to the trees. The figure was still coming toward them. So far, he seemed to be alone.

Kimberly tried to remain calm, yet poised for escape. Then, with a crack of breaking branches, the figure emerged from the trees.

Kimberly let out a whoosh of air. The guy wasn't a Tower twin. He wore wire-rimmed glasses, chinos, and a loosened tie that peeked out from the opening of his green wool jacket. Sandy-blond hair flopped down his forehead onto his glasses. He was slightly good-looking in a very refined, intellectual way.

"Hello. I'm so glad to see someone," he began politely. "I'm in kind of a jam. I was beginning to think I'd be wandering in the forest until I dropped."

At that moment, a coyote howled off in the distance. The horses neighed and reared back fearfully. "No, this isn't a good place to be wandering around alone," Faith stated the obvious. "What happened?"

"My car broke down just off the road up there," he explained, pointing behind him. Then he switched direction and pointed over their shoulders. "Or is it over there? I'm afraid I'm not sure anymore." Perplexed, he swiped at his shaggy, too-long bangs, wiping them away from his face. "You see, I saw a sign for the Tower Ranch and thought I could get help from someone there. I went in the main gate and started walking, and somehow I wound up here. Is this still the Tower Ranch?"

Kimberly looked at Faith. "We hope not."

"Can you ride a horse?" Faith asked him.

The guy glanced at the horses nervously. "No, I'm afraid not. It's the car or my own two legs that get me where I'm going."

"He could hop on behind one of us," Kimberly suggested.

"How about it?" Faith asked him. "Can you manage that?"

The guy looked back at the trees he'd just left. "I don't have much choice." He approached

Faith's horse cautiously. "How does one . . . uh . . . get on?"

"Didn't you ever see any old cowboy movies?" Kimberly teased. "You run toward the back of the horse, then you leap up into the air and land on its back."

"You're joking," he said, turning pale. "Or I hope you are."

"She's joking," Faith assured him. "We've been using the grab-on-and-squirm-your-way-up method. It's not too graceful, but it gets you in the saddle, so to speak."

Faith climbed onto the gray horse and then extended her hand. Nervously, the young man took it. "Well, I can't just pull you up myself," Faith complained. "You have to climb."

Kimberly worked hard not to laugh as the stranger ineffectually kicked up at the horse again and again. Once he lost hold of Faith's hand and fell flat on his back in the wet grass. Gamely he got back up and grabbed Faith's hand, nearly pulling her off in the process.

"This isn't working," Faith observed after putting up with almost five minutes of his fruitless efforts.

"No, wait," he said. "I'll try the Roy Rogers method." Backing up, he pocketed his glasses, then scrunched his face into an expression of fierce determination. With his head down, he began to run toward the side of the horse. His flying leap brought him up high enough for Faith to grab the seat of his pants and help him scramble the rest of the way up.

"And the judges give it a zero for artistic style and a two for technical merit. But at least you're up!" Kimberly teased. Then, handing Faith the rope to the black horse, Kimberly climbed back onto the white and brown mare. "The road is that way across the field," she said, pointing. "Once we're back on the road, I'm sure we'll find your car."

"Shouldn't we just get to a phone and call a towing service?"

"Not unless you know what's wrong with it," Faith said.

The guy laughed glumly. "I don't know one thing about cars."

"Well, I know a little," said Kimberly. "Let's take a look at it. Maybe it's something simple."

They rode across the field and up toward the road. From there, they followed the road back to the car. It was a nondescript, banged-up, cream-colored sedan splotched with patches of rust. Its front bumper hung precariously and there was a spray of spiderweb-fine cracks on the front window. "How far did you drive that wreck?" Faith asked.

He laughed. "How did you know it was a Rent-a-Wreck?" the young man asked.

"Because I have two eyes," Faith said. "Are you serious about the name of the rental company?"

"Absolutely."

"It sure lives up to its name," Kimberly commented.

"To tell the truth, it didn't give me any trouble until now. I drove it all the way from Yale," he told them.

"You drove this thing from the East Coast to Montana?" Faith yelped in disbelief. "You must be desperate to get out here. What's so important?"

"I'm writing a paper on the impact of the new rush of tourism on Montana," he replied. "It's an overdue final paper. If I don't write it, my grade will really suffer."

"Tell me about overdue, last-minute papers," Faith moaned, getting off her horse and tying her to a nearby tree. Kimberly did the same. When all the horses were tied, Kimberly climbed into the front seat of the car. She turned the key, which was still in the ignition. With a sputter, the engine came to life.

"That wasn't too tough," Faith said, leaning in the open driver's door.

"It might have just overheated," Kimberly speculated. She turned to the guy, who had climbed in on the passenger side. "What's your name, by the way?"

"Oh, excuse me. I'm Casper Reilly."

"I'm Kimberly, and this is Faith. Listen, Casper, did this gauge here do anything weird?" Kimberly asked, tapping the temperature gauge.

"Yes, it kept climbing, but I didn't know what that meant."

"It meant something is wrong with your cooling system," Kimberly said. She glanced at his backseat, which was loaded with suitcases, a fax machine, a large sturdy briefcase with the logo of a computer company on it, and a stack of books. "Traveling light, I see," she commented.

Casper shrugged. "What can I say? I'm a prisoner of the electronic age. I'm a modern guy."

"Well, they invented the car at the turn of the century. You seemed to have missed that innovation," she said, laughing. She'd never met a guy who didn't know how to read a temperature gauge. "Listen, how much farther are you traveling?"

"I'm headed for the Angel Dude Ranch. Do you know it?"

Kimberly and Faith looked at each other again and grinned. "As it turns out, we do," Kimberly said. "Just follow us."

Three

The next morning, Winnie sat at the front desk, looking down at her bare toes and whispering into the phone. "Last night I wrote, 'I love Josh,' on my toes in red nail polish, one letter on each toe," she was saying to Josh. "That meant one toe was left over, so I tried to put in an exclamation point, but it was the small toe, so it kind of filled up the whole nail. I suppose I should have stuck to a simple period, but an exclamation point is more fitting. I love you, Josh. And I miss you like anything."

"Me, too. It's weird being here without you," Josh said on the other end.

"I feel like some kind of amoeba, all mushy, like, I don't know exactly who I am without you," Winnie rambled on. "But I'm determined to show everyone here that motor-mouthed flaky Winnie is gone. I'm sick of Faith and KC thinking of me as the original weirdo, you know, ding-dong Winnie. One good thing is that next to Liza, I look totally normal. She makes me look like Princess Poise and Grace."

Josh laughed the warm, comforting laugh that Winnie loved so much. "Don't get too normal on me, Princess Grace. I want the same Winnie I left. The one I married, for better or worse."

"Oooohhh! I love you so much!" Winnie purred. "You are the most lovable, most wonderful, most—" Winnie cut herself off as she checked her Day-Glo green plastic watch. "Geez, we've been on the phone five minutes already! I can't believe it. I'd better get off. I don't want to run up Mrs. Angeletti's bill."

"Oh, Win, I wish I was there. I'll call you next time."

"Okay. I'll be waiting. How's the baby, by the way?"

"She's a baby. Cute and all. But not as cute as you. 'Bye until tomorrow."

Winnie kissed into the phone with a long smack. "'Bye. I love, love, love you."

As she hung up, Winnie smelled the delicious aroma of warm pancakes. "Come and get breakfast while it's hot!" Mrs. Angeletti called to her from the dining-room doorway.

"Be right there," Winnie called back. She propped her head on her hands and sighed. It was hard being away from Josh, but this trip was really important. For one thing, KC needed her. And even though there had been tough times in their friendship over the last several months, they were still best friends. No amount of personality differences and little quibbles could change that. KC and Faith were the sisters only-child Winnie always wished she had. Even if your sister decided to become a super-together hard-boiled businesswoman as KC had—a decision you didn't think much of—she was still your sister.

And then there was project New Winnie. She was seriously determined to upgrade her image by being super-helpful and together on this trip. Lately she'd had a faint, irritating sensation that Faith and KC had bonded in a way that somehow excluded her. Not that they ever overtly left her out; it was more subtle than that. It was as if they had an unstated idea that they were the capable ones, the ones who would achieve something with their lives. Winnie resented it and vowed that she was going to change all that. Winnie the space-case was about to become the captain of the *Enterprise.*

She got up and went into the large dining room, which was a huge, high-ceilinged log room complete with a massive stone fireplace. On the walls, stuffed heads of deer, moose, and elk looked down at her, and in the corner loomed a full-sized stuffed grizzly bear.

The first thing I'd do is get rid of the heads, Winnie thought with a shudder. But other than that, Winnie loved everything about the ranch. It was so rustic that she almost felt like a pioneer woman.

The rest of her friends were already seated at a long table near the door. With them was Casper, looking very preppy in his plain blue button-down shirt and dark-green cardigan sweater.

"Josh says hi to everyone," Winnie told them as she took a seat and poured syrup on her pancakes. "This breakfast looks—and smells—totally great!"

"Well, we promised our guest gourmet meals," Mrs. Angeletti said, smiling at Casper.

"You sure did," KC said as she perused her mother's new color brochure. "And top-notch skiing and horseback riding, and outdoor adventures guided by professionals."

Winnie leaned over to get a look. "Really impressive!"

"Thanks, Winnie," Mrs. Angeletti said. "It had better be. I spent a small fortune on it."

"Your brochure was included with the tourism packet on Montana that I received," Casper told her.

"I hope it's what you expected," Mrs. Angeletti said.

Casper laughed. "It's better. You didn't say I'd be surrounded by a bevy of beautiful women at my very first breakfast."

Winnie cast a sidelong glance at Casper, wondering what he was really doing here. Faith had told her he was here to work on a paper about Montana, but Winnie found that hard to believe. Regular people, even good students, would go to the library and take out books on Montana. They might even write to the chamber of commerce. But they didn't spend Christmas break by themselves in Montana just to do research.

"Did the ranch just open?" Casper asked.

"Yes," KC's mother replied. "I guess it was a little premature. There's quite a bit more work to be done than I expected."

"That's why we're here," Winnie said brightly. "Just point us in the right direction. I'm ready to paint, decorate, chop wood, shovel snow, clean out the stable—you name it."

Mrs. Angeletti nodded. "There's all that to do

and more. When you finish eating, I'll give you all the grand tour. You'll see for yourselves how enormous the task is."

Just then the phone rang, and Mrs. Angeletti left to answer it. "Your mom doesn't seem too shook up by what happened yesterday," Kimberly observed from the other side of the table.

"Mom's real good at covering up," KC said as she poured herself a cup of coffee. "She's tough, too. It's not easy to rattle her."

When they finished breakfast, Mrs. Angeletti stood up and waved for them to follow her. "Tour time," she announced. "Come with us if you'd like, Casper."

"Thanks, I'd love to."

The night before, they'd each seen the cozy upstairs bedrooms with their white pine walls and Indian-design quilts and curtains. Winnie had volunteered to room with Liza, knowing that no one else relished the idea. It was part of her determination to be the most agreeable, helpful person around.

Their first stop on the tour was the restaurant-style kitchen behind the dining room. "Once we start filling up, I'll need you all to help cook and serve," Mrs. Angeletti said. "KC, since you've worked with me in the restaurant back in Oregon, I'd like you to supervise things in here."

"No problem, Mom."

Winnie wished she could volunteer for kitchen duty, but boiling water was about as far as her cooking skills went—and even then, her mother had the scorched pots to disprove the old adage that *anyone* could boil water. Maybe, though, she could learn by helping KC. She made a note to suggest it.

Next Mrs. Angeletti showed them the chicken coop in back, and walked them through the stable, introducing them by name to her four horses. "I really appreciate your going out after them," she told Kimberly and Faith. "If you hadn't been here, I don't know what I would have done."

"I don't know what I would have done, either," added Casper.

"You'd have managed," Kimberly said.

"Managed to get completely lost, you mean," he countered. "Do you have any ideas about what I should do with that car? I checked the phone book. There are no divisions of Rent-a-Wreck out here."

"I looked at it this morning," Kimberly said. "Your radiator is bone-dry. There's got to be a leak somewhere. We can go into town and see if they have any sealant at the hardware store. I wouldn't try driving it back to Harvard, though."

"Yale," Casper corrected her.

"Whatever," Winnie said. She was impressed

with Kimberly's knowledge of cars, which seemed out of character with someone who was so graceful and feminine. But then again, Kimberly was another of her friends who ranked among the intensely capable of this world—an elite company Winnie was determined to soon join. "Would you teach me about cars?" she asked Kimberly as the group walked toward the sprawling front porch. "I've just decided to be car savvy."

"Make that two who want vehicular knowledge," Casper added.

Kimberly looked from Casper to Winnie. "Sure. But the class will last all of ten minutes. Master Mechanic Kimberly Dayton does not know all that much."

Arriving at the porch, the group seated themselves on benches and wooden chairs all around Mrs. Angeletti. "Do any of you have a particular job you'd like to do?" she asked.

"Can I work with the horses?" Faith asked.

"That would be wonderful," Mrs. Angeletti agreed.

"I could put together a winter-sports program for you," Kimberly volunteered. "I ski and I've done some winter camping. I know how to work a snowmobile."

"I think you've just found your trained professional, Mom," KC said.

Her mother smiled. "Thank goodness. Or my brochure wouldn't be telling the truth."

"I'll do whatever needs doing," Winnie said gamely.

"Me, too," Liza spoke up, shifting uncomfortably on her wooden porch chair. She wished she had some special skill to offer like Faith, Kimberly, and KC did. They were so confident. And even though Winnie had nothing special to do, Liza envied her her self-assurance. She also envied Winnie and the close friendship she had with the other girls. *How wonderful it would be to feel included*, Liza thought.

She'd never known what it was like to really belong to a group. That was the main reason, aside from fleeing boredom in her parents' vacation condo in Florida, that she'd wanted to come along on this trip. She wanted to be part of this gang of friends. If they would all just accept her—as they did one another—then maybe she wouldn't have to try so hard to be sexy or famous or funny. She could just be herself—not that she was completely sure of who that might be, but she could begin to find out.

"So, now you've seen it all," said Mrs. Angeletti. "Is there anything else anyone would like to know?"

"I noticed a room right off the dining area," said Casper. "What is that?"

"That's an old bar called the Lazy Q," Mrs. Angeletti told him. "This place was a hotel for a brief period in the fifties, and it was built then. I'm not quite sure yet what I'm going to do with that space."

"Why not turn it back into a bar?" Liza suggested. "You could get an old jukebox, too."

"That's a brilliant idea!" Winnie cried. "Drinks and music always draw a big crowd."

"I don't know," Mrs. Angeletti said, sighing. "Running a bar is a big undertaking. You girls are minors, so I'd have to serve."

"But you know, Mom, a bar could be good for business and . . . um . . . public relations, if you know what I mean," KC said.

Mrs. Angeletti's eyes suddenly widened thoughtfully. "The public-relations aspect is a good point. And if they came in to drink, they might stay to eat."

"And to dance and see shows!" Liza added excitedly. She knew Mrs. Angeletti was taking the idea seriously now that KC had given her support. But it didn't matter. Liza realized that she did have something special to offer. "I could revive the Lazy Q into the hottest spot in Towerton," she went on. "I mean, how much competition could there be in this dinky town? That Hungry Horse isn't exactly Le Club. The Lazy Q could soar. The name might have to get nixed, though. How about The Vixen-Head? You could move in one of those deer heads and it would be a double-entendre kind of thing. It could be a swinging-singles-out-west sort of place."

"Liza," Faith said, a doubtful tone in her voice, "don't get carried away."

"I know I could do it," Liza insisted. "I'm the perfect person for the job. I'm a drama major. I know about theater and comedy. Didn't I win the cable-TV comedy contest?"

"You could have a comedy night," Winnie agreed. "Folks around here could probably use a few laughs."

Liza smiled. She was liking Winnie more and more every second.

"Something tells me the people in Towerton don't have a sense of humor," KC said dryly.

"Okay, maybe you're right, KC," Liza conceded. "But everybody likes music. I'll go down to The Hungry Horse and advertise for local musicians. There's got to be all sorts of singing-cowboy types around here. I might discover a country-singing hunk like Billy Ray Cyrus."

"Cute city, yeah," Winnie sighed.

"It's a wonderful idea, Liza," Mrs. Angeletti said. "But I can't afford to pay even a single musician, let alone a whole band."

Liza frowned. This was too good an idea to let go of. "What about a pass-the-hat kind of thing? You know, an entertainer who would play for tips —and maybe supper?"

"When I was young, folksingers used to work like that all the time," Mrs. Angeletti recalled. "I wouldn't mind feeding them, either." She folded her arms and then unfolded them, obviously weighing the possibilities. "I just got a liquor license, so that I can serve alcohol with dinner and lunch. And the bar is still stocked with glasses. They're very old-fashioned."

"That'll only lend atmosphere," Casper said.

All right, Casper! thought Liza, grateful for the support. *Maybe you're not such a buttoned-up dweeb, after all!*

"I'll tell you what," Mrs. Angeletti said. "If you can manage to find some free entertainment, I'll open the Lazy Q."

"Yes!" Liza cheered.

Now they would all see what Liza Ruff could really do!

Four

An hour later, KC stood by the front desk and banged on the call bell impatiently. "I'm leaving!" she shouted. "Anybody who wants to come, now's the time!"

Winnie clattered down the wooden steps, untying a bandanna from her hair. "Wait for me," she shouted. "I just finished waxing the upstairs floors. You should see them. They're like mirrors."

Liza stepped out of the dining room holding a poster-size roll of paper. "I'm done," she sang out. She unfurled one of the sheets. *Sing for your supper!* it read. *Earn instant fame and awesome tips!!!*

A great opportunity at Towerton's hottest new club!!!
Call Liza with a Z at the Angel Dude Ranch!

"It's catchy," said KC. "But it's not exactly true. I don't know how awesome the tips will be, or if this is exactly the spot to be discovered in."

"A little poetic license never hurt," Liza said, unfazed. "Think positive. This joint will jump, once the Lazy Q opens up. It'll be stupendous! Awesome! Musicians nationwide will be begging to play here."

KC smiled. She hoped Liza was right. "Are you coming out to find a Christmas tree with us?" she asked.

"Wow! I forgot all about it!" Liza cried. She looked back into the dining room hesitantly. "I suppose I can leave my markers and stuff on the table till I get back."

"Why not?" Winnie asked as she zipped up her multicolored parka with its swirling pattern. "You've left your other junk all over our room. Why not spread out!"

Liza rolled her eyes and sighed. "I'm in the throes of creativity," she offered as an explanation. "I can't worry about tidiness when I'm trying to give birth to a compelling advertising campaign. Single-handedly—I might add."

"Yeah, well, we've all been single-handedly busting our butts for a day and a half," Winnie countered. "I don't think drawing posters is exactly backbreaking."

"You don't understand how draining creativity can be," Liza dismissed her. "Not many people do, but—"

KC couldn't stand to hear them argue another moment. "I'm going," she interrupted, heading for the door. "Maybe you can bicker on the way, instead."

"That's possible," Liza said. She smiled at Winnie, then at KC.

KC sighed. "I'm so relieved to hear that. Follow me."

Outside, Kimberly sat on the porch, sanding an American Flyer sled. "Wow, that looks like a lot of work," KC remarked as she watched Kimberly throwing all her energy into the job.

"I'm getting sandpaper hands," Kimberly said. "I don't know if I'm still glad I found these five old sleds and skis in the shed." The paint on them was blistered and peeled, but Kimberly had seen their potential. She'd spent all of yesterday waxing the skis. Today, she was sanding down the sleds for repainting.

Kimberly put down the sled and sandpaper. "Is it tree time?" she asked. "That's one activity I don't want to miss."

"Yep," KC answered. "Where's Faith?"

"Here I am," Faith called as she hurried out of the stable. "I'm ready."

"The ax is right here," said Kimberly, picking up the tool leaning against the porch railing. "I sharpened it this morning."

"Then let's move out," KC said, leading the way to her mother's four-wheel-drive pickup parked by the front door. She climbed behind the wheel, with Winnie and Liza by her side. Kimberly and Faith sat behind, in the truck bed. Just as she turned the key in the ignition, KC spotted Casper running up.

"Where are you all headed?" he asked.

"Christmas-tree hunting," KC informed him. "Want to come?"

"Well, if you wouldn't mind, I'd love to."

"Hop in the back, then." When he was in, KC headed out past the stable, over the grazing land and toward the forest. As the pickup bumped along, KC checked over her shoulder to see how Faith, Kimberly, and Casper were doing in the back. Whatever Kimberly had just said had obviously struck Casper as hysterically funny. He was laughing so hard he had to take off his glasses and wipe the tears from his eyes.

"What do you think of Casper?" Winnie asked.

"He seems nice," KC said, not having given him much thought. To her he was a guest, so she was thrilled that he was there. Beyond that, he just seemed like an ordinary, studious guy, someone she might know from one of her business classes.

"What kind of person spends the holidays by himself just so he can write a school paper?" Liza questioned, wrinkling her nose at the idea.

"A devoted one, I guess," said KC. "Maybe he has no family."

"Not even friends?" Liza pressed. "That's odd, if you ask me."

"Some people are loners," KC observed.

"Yeah, like serial killers," said Liza. "When news reporters interview some psycho-creep's neighbors, they say, 'He was always so quiet and kept to himself.'"

Winnie turned sharply and looked out the back window. "I don't think Casper is a psycho killer," she decided after a moment. "He's social with us. And he does seem nice."

"Famous last words," Liza intoned dramatically.

KC stopped the pickup by a bank of fir trees and turned off the engine. "Mom said this is probably the best spot."

"There sure are enough trees to choose from," Liza agreed.

The sharp, crisp cold made KC shiver as she stepped out from the warm cab. "No wonder they call this Big Sky country," she said, taking in the majestic sweep of blue above her.

"This is the most beautiful place I've ever seen." Faith inhaled, climbing out of the pickup. "Every time you turn around, the view is more breathtaking than the one before it. I wonder if people who've always lived around here take it for granted."

"I guess you get used to it after a while," said Kimberly as they all began to walk toward the forest.

Suddenly, KC threw up her arms. "Great woodspeople we are! We forgot the ax!"

"I'll go get it," Casper volunteered. He turned and sprinted back toward the truck.

"Do you think it's wise to let him have the ax?" Liza joked. "A sharp blade in the wrong hands—"

"Let's drop that. It's not funny anymore," KC said, frowning. "Anyway, I say if Casper has the ax, maybe he'll chop down the tree for us."

"KC!" Faith chided. "I can't believe you said such a sexist thing."

"Sorry." KC smiled sheepishly as Casper came back with the ax. She took the lead as they went into the pine trees. KC was intent on finding the most perfect tree. Every year until now her father had cut down a tree for the family. With a pang of sadness, KC realized she had the feeling that she'd be letting her father down if she didn't meet his high standards.

Looking around in all directions, they began searching for the perfect tree to stand in the lobby of the Angel Dude Ranch. One after another, they rejected them: too skinny, too lopsided, too square.

"How about that one," KC suggested. Standing alone in a patch of sunlight was a triangular tree, about eight feet tall.

"It's perfect!" Faith cried.

KC nodded. She could easily imagine her father dragging this tree off the top of the family car. This tree made the grade. "I think it's the one," she told the others.

"Let me have a whack at it," Kimberly said, taking the ax from Casper. Everyone stood back as she swung the ax, sinking the blade into the tree with a thud. She chopped at different angles, creating a V of light wood near the base.

"Kimberly, where did you learn to do that?" KC asked, impressed with Kimberly's expertise.

"I was a camp counselor," Kimberly said as she landed another blow.

"She fixes cars, she chops trees, she's amazing!" Casper laughed. "Do you want a break, Wonder Woman?"

Kimberly wiped sweat from her brow with the

back of her sleeve and handed him the ax. "Thanks," she panted. "That's all I can handle."

"Aha!" cried Casper. "Your tired. I'm shocked. Could it be you're a real human person, after all?"

"I'm as human as they come, believe me," Kimberly said, looking into Casper's eyes.

KC noticed that Casper was looking right back. Was there some attraction between Kimberly and Casper? KC wasn't sure. She just knew that Casper was humming as he finished cutting the tree, which crashed to the ground with a loud thud. It took all of them to carry it to the pickup and throw it into the back.

Just as they were brushing pine needles from their jackets, Mrs. Angeletti rode up on the gray mare named Cloudy. KC looked at her mother, whose wisps of dark, gray-flecked hair had come loose from her thick braid and framed her strong, attractive face. A funny thing was happening, KC noticed. Since she'd arrived, her mother's appearance seemed different to her. She looked smaller than KC recalled, yet prettier, too. For the first time in KC's life, her mother didn't have all the answers. Of course, there had been many times when KC hadn't agreed with her mother's answers, yet her mother had been sure they were the right ones. There had been some comfort in that. Now something very real had changed inside her mother. KC wasn't sure what it was, and it made her uneasy.

"How are you guys doing?" Mrs. Angeletti called.

"We found a real beauty," Winnie told her happily. "I can't wait to decorate it."

"A beauty it is," Mrs. Angeletti agreed, looking at the tree. "But now how are all of you planning to fit in the truck?"

"We didn't think of that." KC admitted.

Mrs. Angeletti got down off her horse. "I have an idea. Faith, why don't you ride someone back on Cloudy. KC, would you mind walking with me? I want to talk to you about a few things."

KC didn't like the expression on her mother's face. It was something that hadn't changed. She'd seen it before. It was an expression of forced cheerfulness. "Sure," KC said, throwing Kimberly the keys.

"Can I get on the back with you?" Liza asked Faith, who had already climbed onto Cloudy. "I've never ridden before."

Faith extended a hand. "Climb up."

"See you guys back at the ranch," Kimberly said as she got into the cab with Casper and Winnie. From the corner of her eye, KC noticed Casper scoot in front of Winnie. KC wondered if he had done that in order to sit next to Kimberly. *Poor guy*, she thought. *He's not her type at all. He's in for a letdown.*

Waving at the others, KC began to walk with her mother. The damp grass squooshed under her hiking boots and the sky overhead had begun to cloud over. Mrs. Angeletti walked with her arms folded, looking lost in thought.

"What's the matter, Mom?" KC asked. "I know something is wrong."

Her mother smiled sadly. "Is it that obvious?"

"Only to me," KC replied. "When you fold your arms and forget to talk, I know you're worried."

"Well, you're right," Mrs. Angeletti admitted. "That's what I wanted to talk to you about, too. I want you to know what's really happening with the ranch."

"Which is what?" KC asked gently.

"To put it bluntly, I'm broke. Just the initial repairs on the lodge ate up all the life-insurance money and the profit from selling The Windchime. If I hadn't gotten an emergency loan from a wonderful young banker in Towerton, I might not have been able to open at all. Thanks to her I was able to sink a new well when the old one's water was found to be undrinkable."

"But now everything's fixed, isn't it?" asked KC.

"Yes, until the next disaster. I have no backup money if anything goes wrong. And I was counting on making my loan payments from the money I earned from the guests."

"But, so far, there are no guests—or at least not enough," KC said, following her mother's drift.

Her mother put her arm around KC as they walked. For a moment, it felt like everything was back to normal—like the old days when KC felt sheltered and safe with her mother's arm around her. But KC had to remind herself things weren't normal. Her father was gone. If things had been normal, he was the one her mother would have leaned on. But he was dead. It was incredibly hard to face, but this made it very real. He wasn't there to help, so KC had to be.

KC had always thought of herself as being more practical than either of her parents, especially her mother. Now was the time to tap into that practicality and come up with some realistic answers. *Think,* she urged herself.

"If only I had some savings left," Mrs. Angeletti sighed.

"What about Grandma Rose?" KC suggested. "She'll always be there for you. And you said she gave you the ranch. I know she wants this place to do well."

Mrs. Angeletti shook her head. "I can't ask her. She's already been too generous. I've got to do the rest on my own."

"I'd probably feel the same." KC searched her brain for another idea. There had to be something her mother could do. She tried to remember if there had been anything in her marketing course that might be helpful.

"Could you get the help of downtown business owners?" KC asked, recalling what she knew about public relations. "You know, that way if anyone came into town and asked for a good place to stay, they'd direct them here."

Instantly her mother's eyes brimmed with tears.

"Mom, what is it?" KC asked, alarmed. "Did I say something wrong?"

Mrs. Angeletti brushed away the tears with the heels of her hands. "I'm sorry," she said in a choked voice. "It just all seems like too much. I can't face a whole town that hates me."

"What are you talking about?" KC put an arm around her mother's shoulders and squeezed her tight. "Did something happen?"

"I met one of the Tower twins in the feed store yesterday. I confronted him about setting the horses free. He looked at me, cold as ice, and said I was a know-nothing city bloodsucker, and that people like me were ruining the entire state."

"That's absurd!" KC cried angrily. "Did anyone else hear him?"

"Yes, and that's the part that really disturbs me.

When Jake Tower left, I went to pay for my supplies. The man behind the counter wouldn't even meet my eyes. I felt like he agreed with him."

"Could you have a talk with Old Man Tower?" KC suggested. "Maybe if you confronted him it would help. They have no right to do this to you. You have to insist that they stop."

KC was so outraged that she felt as if she couldn't breathe. How dare they do this! It was so unfair! In all her life KC had never seen her mother do a mean thing to anyone. Why were they picking on her? Her mother's entire future was at stake here.

Mrs. Angeletti gazed at KC a moment. "You're so like your father in some ways. If he were here he'd have stormed up to the Tower Ranch and demanded to talk to Tower." Tears spilled from her eyes. "Why isn't he here now? It's not fair that I should have to do this by myself."

KC hugged her mother, feeling the tears begin to well in her own eyes. "You're not by yourself, Mom. I'm here. I won't let you down."

She held her mother tightly again and let her cry. KC blinked back her own tears. How many times had she cried in her mother's arms? She couldn't even count them. Now it was her turn to be strong.

What good were all the business courses she'd taken if they couldn't serve her now? In her mind, she began running through all she'd learned about accounting, advertising, and public relations.

She felt a fierceness inside her that she'd never experienced before. They wouldn't break her mother with their mean-spiritedness. KC would help her mother fight with everything she had inside her. Her mother would win, too. KC couldn't accept any other outcome.

"I have an idea," KC said as her mother wiped her eyes. "We'll give a big dinner for the local merchants. Once they meet you and know what you're about, they'll be won over."

"Do you think so?"

"Sure. Who could ever resist you? The food will knock 'em dead, and maybe Liza will even have found some musicians by then."

A flicker of a smile flashed across Mrs. Angeletti's face, then faded. "I can't do it," she said. "No money. Remember?"

"My finance teacher says you should stay in touch with your creditors. Let them know what's happening instead of just missing payments. Can we talk to that banker you liked so much? I mean, is she approachable?"

Mrs. Angeletti began walking again. "Suzanna is very human. I could try talking to her. Maybe she can give me a grace period before my first payment is due."

"That's the spirit," KC cheered.

Her mother squeezed her hand.

They walked on quietly until the lodge came into view. Suddenly, Mrs. Angeletti stopped dead. "What's that on the stable?"

KC followed her gaze and saw a splash of red on the side of the barn facing them. Her mother was already running toward the lodge. KC broke into a run behind her.

When she caught up with her mother she saw what had happened. Someone had scrawled an obscenity across the side of the barn in bold red paint. Under it were the words: GO HOME!

"They won't win, Mom," KC said angrily. "No matter what it takes. We won't let the Towers win!"

Five

············

*L*iza looked out the back window as Kimberly's van bumped along the dirt road away from the Angel Dude Ranch the next morning. Her handmade posters advertising for musical groups to play at the Lazy Q lay on the floor at her feet. The van was quiet as each of the girls sat wrapped in her own thoughts.

It's funny how people establish their spots right off and then stick to them, Liza thought, noting that they had settled into the exact same seating arrangement as when they arrived. Kimberly and KC were in the front, Faith and Winnie behind them, and Liza was in the back. It was as if some sort of unconscious pecking order of power and authority was being played out here in the van.

Liza wasn't shocked by the realization that she was last in line. She knew it. She wasn't athletic and graceful like Kimberly, or gorgeous and pulled-together like KC. Nor was she as pretty and likable as Faith. She wasn't even cute and bubbly like Winnie. But she knew her own good qualities, even if the others couldn't see them. She was a talented actress with a flare for comedy. And maybe she wasn't a beauty, but that wasn't going to make her hide in the shadows. Just the opposite. She was who she was, so why not light it up in neon clothing? Why not go all out with it? There were other actresses who had forced the world to see their unique beauty—Barbra Streisand, Bette Midler, Liza Minelli. They believed in their own beauty, and eventually convinced everyone else. That's what Liza hoped to do.

The quality Liza most liked about herself was her tenacity. She hung on and hung on and never gave up. That was the quality that would make the Lazy Q a success. And when the Lazy Q was working, they'd all look at her in a new light. Liza wasn't sure who she would supplant in the pecking order, but she knew she would be moving up very soon.

Before long Kimberly was driving on the sloping

road leading into downtown Towerton. To the right was a village green with a large bronze statue of a cowboy. He appeared to be riding at full gallop. *He's cute,* Liza smiled to herself as Kimberly pulled to the curb. *Too bad he can't sing.*

"All right. I'll meet you all right back here in an hour," Kimberly said as they climbed out of the van.

Liza got out and looked down the road at Main Street, Towerton. At ten in the morning, it was as if the town hadn't come fully awake yet. Only a few people crossed the street, and there weren't many cars. It was another gray day, with the kind of damp cold that made Liza's mane of red hair frizz.

"Let's go," Winnie said, coming around the front of the van with Faith and KC. "Operation Angel Invasion is about to begin."

"Angel Invasion—that's a good name for a band," said Liza. The day before, KC had called an emergency meeting to mobilize them for action. She was excited and determined to make the merchants' dinner she had planned a roaring success.

The plan today was for Liza and Winnie to tack up the posters and shop for groceries they'd need, while Faith and KC hand-delivered invitations to the merchants. Kimberly would go off to scout out local skating spots for their "winter adventure" potential. Winnie had dubbed the undertaking "Operation Angel Invasion."

"See you guys," KC said, waving, as she and Faith went off down the street.

Liza waved back. "There they go," she said to Winnie. "It must be great to be so perfect."

"What do you mean?" asked Winnie.

"Don't they get on your nerves sometimes? Just a little? They both have such a superior way about them. It's kind of annoying. Their hair doesn't even frizz in this weather."

Winnie ran her fingers through her own short, brown spiky hair. "Neither does mine, but that's because it's loaded with gel."

Liza looked at Winnie in her purple sweats layered with a heavy quilted pink down vest. Her plastic red Crayola crayon earrings bobbed from her ears. She wasn't like Faith and KC. She was looser, quirkier. At least she was someone Liza could relate to.

"I know what you mean about Faith and KC," Winnie said as they began walking down the street. Liza scurried along in her fur-trimmed high-heel boots, finding it hard to keep up with her. "But they're my oldest friends. We went to high school together," Winnie went on. "I'm used to them. I guess we can all be irritating in our own ways."

"I suppose. I know I irritate the hell out of Faith," said Liza, breathless from walking so fast. "She thinks I'm too dramatic, but she's a theater major herself. You'd think she'd understand the theatrical temperament. Then again, she's a behind-the-scenes person. A lot of the technical people disdain actors."

"Faith doesn't disdain actors," Winnie disagreed. "She has friends who want to be center stage. And look how involved she got with Alec Brady. She didn't feel contempt for him."

"Oh, well, that's different," Liza squealed. "Who wouldn't want to be involved with Alec Brady?"

"I know!" Winnie said, stooping to retie a lace of her red sneakers. "It must have been so exciting. He even gave her his private number and told her to call him any time."

"You're kidding," Liza cried. Why couldn't things like that happen to her? "I would die. I would just die! I'd be calling him every second of the day. Oh! Could you imagine?"

"Faith hasn't called him once," Winnie said, as she straightened up. "Faith *is* cool, there's no denying that. Too cool sometimes, I know. It can get annoying. But KC is even cooler."

"You said it. KC is so cool she almost seems like an icicle."

"I wouldn't go that far," Winnie said, walking on as quickly as before. "Inside she feels very passionately about things. She's a very private person. You just have to get to know her."

"Is that possible?" Liza asked doubtfully as she hurried alongside Winnie once again. "Does anyone really know her?"

"I do," Winnie said confidently. "Other people do too. But it isn't easy. It takes KC a long time to trust people. I'm not sure why. Give it time."

Liza wished she didn't care what Faith and KC thought of her. But she did. Maybe because part of her—a part she wasn't overly fond of—wanted to be just like them. And that fact made them even more annoying to her.

Liza reached out and grabbed hold of Winnie's arm. "Could you slow down? Where are we rushing to, anyway?"

"The supermarket," Winnie replied. "Isn't it about five blocks down this way?"

"Yeah, but wouldn't it make more sense to hang up my posters as we go along?" Liza suggested as she caught her breath. "We'll pass The Hungry Horse. I want to put up my first poster there. The sparkle stuff on it is getting all over my jacket." As she spoke she brushed multicolored sparkles from her bright-orange parka.

"Hey, look!" Winnie said, pointing to the sign

above the movie theater right in front of them. "*The Last Ride* is playing."

"Isn't that Alec Brady's new movie?" Liza said, trying to recall what she'd read in *People*.

"Yep. I'll have to tell Faith," said Winnie excitedly. Liza followed Winnie a few feet over to the theater, the front of which looked as if it had remained unchanged since the 1920s. Two fat Roman columns ornately decorated with cherubs on top flanked the now-empty glass ticket booth. Liza and Winnie studied the movie poster to the left of the columns. Alec Brady stood in front of a massive, curling wave, dressed in surfing trunks, clutching his surfboard in one hand and a pistol in the other. *The last ride is always the wildest!* the tag line on the poster teased.

Liza sighed and tried to imagine what it would be like to be personal friends with a star. Alec Brady was so sexy, with his muscular physique and action-ready stance. His hair was cut very short, setting off his intense eyes. He seemed—as Liza's acting teacher would say—centered and in touch with his deepest animal self.

"This movie looks kind of dumb, but I'd go see Alec Brady anytime," Winnie said.

"Let's go some night," agreed Liza. "There isn't much else to do after eight P.M."

Diagonally across the street was The Hungry

Horse. "Come on," said Liza as they crossed. "I have the feeling this is the center of the local music scene."

They went inside and were greeted by the same moussed-hair waitress who had waited on them before. They showed her their poster and asked if they could hang it. "Well, I thought *this* was the hottest club in town," she said pleasantly. "But I guess we can stand a little competition. Tack it up just around the bend there, by the phone."

Liza led the way. "I'll put it right here by this cute rodeo-rider dude," she said, holding the poster next to the ad for the indoor rodeo.

The poster with the name Lazy Q spelled out in swirling, sparkling letters looked too glitzy next to the spare black-and-white rodeo poster beside it. Liza couldn't help checking out the rider. In some ways, he looked more like a movie star than Alec Brady did. His face was more classically handsome. He also seemed "centered and in touch with his deepest animal self." It showed in his posture and the intensity on his high-boned face. How did he manage to hang on like that? she wondered. The second after that photo was snapped, did he go flying off into the air? Did he slam to the ground on his back and have to be dragged out, barely alive?

Liza decided they wouldn't have used his picture if he had met a grisly death. More likely he was some sort of rodeo hotshot who held on tight and never got hurt. That was what Liza intended on doing—hanging in there and not letting anything hurt her.

"While you hang posters, why don't I start shopping for the groceries we need," Winnie suggested. "You have the list, right?"

Liza snapped her fingers and sighed. "The list! I knew I forgot something! When I changed my jeans I left it in my other pocket."

"Liza! KC and her mom want to try out all the recipes for this big dinner before they serve them for real. Now what are we going to do?"

"Chill, would you?" said Liza. "I remember what they wanted. After all, I'm an actress. I've memorized whole scripts. A dinky little grocery list is nothing."

Winnie fished in her large leather purse for a pen and paper. She dug up a pen, but no paper. "Use the back of this," Liza said, pulling the picture of the handsome rodeo rider off the wall. "I don't want him here, anyway. He'll distract people from my poster, and he's hogging up the center of the board."

Leaning against the wall, Winnie jotted down the ingredients as Liza recited them to her. ". . . and tomatoes. I'm sure that's all of it," Liza said finally.

"I hope so," said Winnie, pocketing the list.

"Whoever finishes first will come find the other one. Okay?"

"Later," Liza chirped as Winnie left. She flattened her poster against the bulletin board and reread it: "Musicians needed at Towerton's newest hot spot. Sing for tips and gourmet meals. Don't miss this chance to make it big!!! Call Liza."

"Brilliant!" she congratulated herself. Surely it would draw all sorts of talent into the Angel Dude Ranch.

She'd just pushed in the last tack when she sensed someone standing behind her. She turned and found herself looking up at a good-looking guy with hair as bright red as her own and a full mustache to match. In his jeans and western shirt, he was well-built and tall. His brown eyes sparkled with amusement as he looked at her.

"Towerton's new hot spot, huh," he chortled, chewing a large wad of gum. "How come I never heard of it?"

"Because it's hot," Liza shot back. "Like the poster says."

"Is that so? It just so happens that I know everything that's going down in the music scene around here."

"Really?" Liza asked skeptically. She tried to assess the truth of his words. He didn't look like the intense, serious musicians she knew. With his open face and laughing eyes, she could more easily picture him driving a tractor or pitching horseshoes at the local fire department. "You're really a musician?" she questioned.

"Really," he assured her cockily. "I'm Billy Gates, known around here as Coyote. They call me that because I can make my guitar wail like a coyote howling at the moon. I happen to be a guitar player supreme."

"If you do say so yourself," Liza said snidely, put off by his arrogance.

"Yes, I do say so, and I'm not the only one." Narrowing his eyes, he studied the poster. "You *are* joking about this tip thing, aren't you?" he sneered. "What does this gig really pay? If it's worth our while, my band and I might just come over and pay you a call."

"You'll have to audition first," Liza told him, laughing as arrogantly as she could. "I'll be the judge of how supreme your guitar playing is."

His upper lip lifted into an amused smirk. "Something tells me you wouldn't know a hot guitar if it licked your nose."

Liza had never felt like slapping a person as much in her life. "Are all the musicians around here as obnoxious as you?" she asked him.

"I'm not obnoxious," he replied, unruffled. "I'm just giving you the facts. When you're the best, you're the best. Why say otherwise?"

He looked into her eyes, and Liza found herself unable to break away from his gaze. "If you're so eager to hire the best band in town, come on down to the Tower Christmas barn dance this weekend and hear my band play," he continued. "We're the Lonely Rangers. The dance is by invitation only, but it's a huge shindig, so no one will notice a few extra guests. A brassy little number like you has probably crashed a few parties in her time."

Liza's shoulders rose angrily. "Who the hell are you calling a brassy number, you . . . you . . . egomaniacal local yokel!" she shouted. With that, she stomped past him, straight out the front door.

"Whoa!" Winnie cried as Liza charged into her, nearly knocking the grocery bags from her arms. "What's wrong?"

"I think we've stumbled into some brainwarped hick mutant zone," Liza ranted. "The people here are either mean, nasty vandals, or they have egos the size of Orca the killer whale."

"What happened?" asked Winnie, struggling under the weight of her packages.

Taking a bag from her, Liza told her all about Billy "Coyote" Gates as they walked along, putting up the rest of the posters.

"Coyote Gates," she fumed while she tacked

another poster up on a laundromat bulletin board. "Whoever heard of a name like that? It's like something out of one of those old grade-B westerns. Coyote! Can you believe it? What a joke!"

When their hour was up, Liza and Winnie met the others as they'd arranged. "Guess what I did," said KC, packing the grocery bags together in the back of the van.

"Met one of the Tower twins and punched his lights out," Liza guessed.

"No. I signed the ranch up for the Winter Carnival Cleanup Committee."

"You what!" cried Winnie.

"It's part of my public-relations campaign," KC explained, her eyes bright with enthusiasm. "It'll impress the other business owners and show the locals that the Angel Dude Ranch is now part of this community. Only one of us has to show up to represent the ranch."

"Which one?" Liza asked.

"Whoever is available," KC said. "I don't care. I'll do it if no one else wants to."

"I think it's a brilliant strategy," Faith backed up KC.

"Couldn't you have signed on to a different committee?" Liza wailed. "Something like the decoration committee, or the entertainment committee?"

"Nope. Cleanup was the only committee that still needed volunteers," KC told her. "Besides, it's perfect for us, because people will really appreciate what we're doing. They'll see we're not just city slickers, that we're willing to do the dirty work."

"Speak for yourself!" Liza objected. "I'm a city slicker and proud of it."

"I found two great skating spots," Kimberly reported. "How did the merchants respond to the invitations?"

"Pretty good," Faith replied. "I could see they were surprised, but no one was rude to us and most of them said they thought they could come."

"This dinner has got to be perfect," KC said, buckling her seat belt. "Did you guys get everything we need for our trial run?"

Liza didn't like the questioning glance Winnie shot her. "Were you able to get everything on the list?" she asked Winnie.

"Yes, as long as everything was *on* the list," Winnie replied pointedly.

"Then, yes, KC, we have everything," Liza said. One thing she was confident about was her memory.

"Terrific," said KC. "Phase two of Operation Angel Invasion is about to begin."

Six

*F*aith pushed a button on the food processor and sent a vivid orange spray of minced carrots splattering inside the covered mixing bowl. The processor's high-pitched whine drowned out the chatter of the other girls as they worked in the kitchen. Inwardly, Faith sighed with relief. The processor's white noise was a relief from all the talking—especially from Liza, who hadn't stopped complaining about Coyote Gates all afternoon. If Faith heard his name one more time she thought she would scream.

A quick glance revealed that the carrots were

liquefying. Reluctantly, Faith shut off the engine and was once again assaulted with the frantic tones of Liza's obsessive ruminations. "I'm sure Coyote isn't nearly as hot as he says," Liza ranted as she chopped celery with an almost frightening vehemence. "To hear him talk you'd think he was Eric Clapton, Hank Wilson, and Alabama all rolled into one super-hick rock star from hell."

"Maybe he's as good as he says," Kimberly said, looking up from the turkey she was basting.

Liza shook her head. "No way, José. If he was really that great he wouldn't have to brag so much. I never met anyone so detestable. Honestly! He was really too much. In a way, I'd like to crash that Tower barn dance just to hear what a bogus musician he really is."

"What's a simmer?" Winnie asked from her spot by the stove. "The recipe says to reduce it to a simmer, but I'm not positive what that means. I mean, I know in theory what it is, but in raw reality, what does it look like?"

KC adjusted the knob on the stove and dipped a clean wooden spoon into Winnie's chestnut soup, stirring gently. "There. I'd say that's a perfect simmer," she said. "The soup looks good, Win."

"Thanks," Winnie replied. "I'm just following directions."

"This bird only needs about another ten minutes," Kimberly announced.

"Great." KC glanced around the kitchen. "Everything else is nearly ready, too. Liza, would you go tell Casper that we'll be ready to eat in about fifteen minutes?"

Liza slid her sliced celery off the cutting board and into the abundantly filled wooden salad bowl. "Sure thing. I shall command the resident friendly ghost to make an appearance."

The moment Liza flounced out the kitchen door, Faith sighed with relief. "Thank God! I thought she'd never shut up about that Coyote character. It's like she gets a big kick out of hating him. Why can't she just forget about him, already?"

Winnie chuckled as she covered her soup. "Don't you see what she's about?"

"Breaking the world record for nonstop talking?" Faith countered dryly.

Winnie laughed. "No. She's got a thing for Coyote. Women don't obsess about men they hate. They obsess about guys they're stuck on."

"Do you think so?" Faith asked, unconvinced. "She *acts* like she hates him."

"Maybe she does, in a way," Winnie said. "But I'll bet you anything she's also attracted to him. We all know opposites attract."

Faith smiled to herself. She knew what Winnie

was talking about. Last semester she'd felt Scott Sills was Mr. Wrong in almost every way—but some inexplicable attraction kept drawing her back to him. And then there was Alec Brady, movie star. The last thing she'd expected was to have a romance with him. He was insufferably arrogant when they first met, and yet the attraction between them was undeniable and couldn't be explained rationally.

"You know, it would serve Liza right if we maneuvered her into a romance with Coyote, the same way she's always playing matchmaker with us. A payback might teach her a lesson."

"How would you go about doing that?" Kimberly asked as she loaded silverware from a drawer into a woven basket.

"I'm not sure," Faith admitted. "Who knows if we'll ever even run into him again."

"If we crash that barn dance, we would," KC said in a low, serious voice.

Faith looked at her friend. She'd seen that expression on her face before—her brows were knit and she was chewing softly on her lower lip. "What are you thinking, KC?"

"That if I could get into that dance, I could talk to Mr. Tower," KC replied pensively. "It's time to open the channels of communication and get this stupid feud done with."

"I don't know," Kimberly objected. "You could make matters worse."

"How could it?" asked Winnie. "It always helps to talk. The dance might be a real kick, too."

"And I'd get a chance to work on hooking up Liza and Coyote," added Faith. "Let's do it."

Just then, Liza came swinging in through the door. "Do what?" she asked.

"Crash the Tower barn dance," KC told her.

"Yes!" Liza cheered. "That's the spirit, you guys. We need a good adventure!"

Faith looked at KC. As she expected, KC wasn't smiling. "This isn't an adventure," she said to Liza. "This is serious business."

Winnie placed the last serving dish on the dining room table just as Casper walked in. "Wow! It smells great in here," he said, brushing his sandy bangs away from his face. "Mrs. Angeletti will have those merchants begging to be her best friend after this meal."

"Make way for the turkey," Kimberly sang as she backed out of the kitchen, buckling a bit under the weight of the large bird on the tray.

"I'll help you with that," said Casper, sprinting over to assist her. Together, they placed the tray in the center of the table. "I'm sure lucky," he continued. "I'll be the first to sample the gourmet cooking promised by the brochure."

"Wait till you taste my chestnut soup," Winnie said. "You'll die."

"Speaking of waiting," Casper said, shooting a devilish glance at Kimberly, "I'm still waiting for one of the guided outdoor adventures the brochure promised. When are the professional guides showing up?"

"I'm the guide," Kimberly took up his challenge. "I've been a camp counselor, I've taken lots of ski lessons, I have my Red Cross certification in CPR and first aid. I'm as professional as they come."

"Okay, so guide me," he said. "I'm ready anytime you are."

Kimberly scrunched up her face. "I'm still getting myself organized," she demurred. "Besides, there isn't much snow on the ground. Winter activities without snow aren't much fun—if even possible."

"I see your point."

"But," Kimberly said, "when I think of something, you'll be the first to know."

"Thanks." Casper gestured out to the empty room. "I wouldn't want all these tons of other guests to get in line ahead of me."

Kimberly laughed. "No, we wouldn't want that."

Winnie watched them banter. She'd never seen Kimberly look prettier or more animated. Whether or not she was attracted to Casper, Kimberly was enjoying his attention. And Casper never took his eyes off her.

It made Winnie even more homesick for Josh. Friends were wonderful, but she missed feeling special, the way only Josh could make her feel.

Mrs. Angeletti came into the dining room and clapped her hands in delight. "What a feast!" she cried, her dark eyes sparkling happily. "It looks and smells fabulous! Simply fabulous!" Winnie was glad to see her so happy. She couldn't wait for her to taste the chestnut soup. Winnie was so proud of it. Who would think that she could actually make homemade soup? As soon as she got back to Springfield, she'd make a batch for Josh.

"Hopefully it tastes even better than it smells," said KC, coming out of the kitchen with Faith and Liza.

"Well, let's sit down and give it a try," Mrs. Angeletti suggested. With a scratching of chairs against the wood floor, the girls and Casper took their seats. They instantly began to pass the covered white bowls. "I can't decide whether to serve wine as well as cider," Mrs. Angeletti said as she poured herself a glass of cider. "I shy away from wine because I'm not that knowledgeable about it. We didn't serve alcohol at The Windchime."

"I always like a Beaujolais with turkey," Casper recommended.

He what? thought Winnie. She'd never met anyone sophisticated enough to make a statement like that. Who was he? On the one hand, he seemed like your average sort-of-cute college prepster. On the other, he was surprisingly cultivated and even witty.

"I thought only white wine was served with poultry," said Mrs. Angeletti.

"A lot of people think that, but a Beaujolais is considered acceptable with both poultry and red meat," he replied, serving himself some candied yams. "It's a light-bodied red wine, and turkey has a stronger flavor than most poultry, so it can stand up to a red without having its flavor drowned out."

"How do you know so much about wine?" asked Kimberly.

"My father is a real connoisseur," Casper replied. "He goes to wine tastings and the whole bit. He's taught me a few things."

All this talk of wine made Winnie drum her fingers on the table anxiously. The chestnut-soup recipe had called for wine, but there hadn't been any.

At the end of the table, Faith was ladling the steaming brown liquid from the soup tureen as everyone passed their bowls down to her. Winnie watched excitedly.

"This will all go a lot more smoothly when we're serving, of course," said KC. "We should have a dry run for serving, too. Everything has to be perfect."

"Always serve from the left and remove from the right," said Casper.

"Now, how do you know *that*?" asked Kimberly, echoing Winnie's own thoughts.

Casper laughed. "I'm just a fount of invaluable knowledge."

"Well, try the soup, fount," Liza said. "Let's hear your gourmet opinion on that."

All eyes turned to Casper as he dipped his spoon into the soup. Under the table, Winnie wrung her hands and prayed that he would adore it. She pictured him smacking his lips. *C'est magnifique!* he might say as everyone gently applauded.

Let him love it! Let them all love it, she prayed.

But in the next moment, Winnie felt herself go pale. She dug her nails into her palm as Casper coughed and sputtered, growing red in the face. "What is it?" Winnie cried. "What's wrong?"

Casper could only look at her with watery eyes, still coughing.

Curious, the rest of them gingerly took sips from their own soup. "Oh, gross me out!" Liza cried as the others wiped their mouths in disgust.

"Winnie! What did you make this with?" Faith asked, reaching for her glass of cider.

"I . . . I . . . followed the recipe," Winnie said weakly. She lifted her spoon with a trembling hand and brought it to her lips. Winnie sipped. "Oh!" she cried. The taste was indescribably wretched— yet it gave her a clue as to where she had gone wrong.

"It tastes like there's vinegar in this soup," Mrs. Angeletti said. "A lot of vinegar."

"There is," Winnie admitted dismally, wishing she could sink through the wide-planked floor below her.

"Are you crazy? What possessed you to do that?" KC cried.

"The recipe called for chicken broth," Winnie explained apologetically. "But we forgot to buy the broth." She glared meaningfully across the table at Liza, who slunk down guiltily in her chair. Liza's infallible memory had been fallible, after all. The broth had never made it onto the list that Winnie had scrawled on the back of the rodeo poster.

Liza grimaced and sunk lower in her seat.

"The recipe said you could substitute wine,"

Winnie went on, "but we didn't have that, either. Then I found some wine vinegar in the pantry . . . so . . . I figured, wine and wine vinegar. You know. The wine vinegar looked like wine to me. I thought it was close enough. But . . . it wasn't, I guess."

"I guess not," Kimberly said, laughing.

"It's all right. That's why we had this dry run," said Mrs. Angeletti, patting Winnie's hand.

"It's *not* all right!" KC spoke hotly. "Winnie, everything depends on making the dinner a success. Everything! There's no place for Winnie Gottlieb flakiness right now. None!" KC got to her feet. "You can't mess up again."

Winnie fought back hot tears. "I—I won't," she stammered, thinking that although KC was one of her best friends, she really hated her sometimes.

Seven

KC watched the guests flooding into the Towers' barn dance and jammed her hands into the pockets of her gray wool coat. She and her friends were waiting, off to the left of the large red barn. They'd been milling around in the cold for almost a half hour, waiting for the right moment to crash the dance. There was no point in being bounced right out before they were even through the door.

The first step was getting past the cowboy sitting at a card table by the door, checking invitations. His steely gaze and broad shoulders made KC assume he was both welcoming committee and bouncer. He didn't look like the type who could be cajoled into letting them in without invitations.

As of yet, KC had been unable to formulate a plan to get past him.

"Why don't I go around the back and see if there are any side doors or open windows," Faith suggested, pushing back her long hair as the wind whipped it around her face.

"Good idea," said Winnie. "I'll go around the other side and meet you."

As the girls split up and went in opposite directions, Kimberly and Liza continued to sit on the split-rail fence and watch the people arrive. Some, like Kimberly, had parked along the dirt road leading to the barn. Most of the cars were in an adjacent grazing field.

A cowboy with a long blond ponytail and a white Stetson walked past. KC looked at him sharply. Was he Jake Tower? No, she decided upon taking a second look. But perhaps he was the twin, the one she'd seen only dimly in the pouring rain the day they let the horses loose from the barn. KC looked at the guy again as he passed into the barn. He wasn't a Tower. Jake Tower had a weak chin and nasty eyes. There would be no mistaking him or his twin when they met again. And they were bound to. The twins were sure to be here. KC only hoped she could control herself enough not to make a scene, but she would surely let them know what she thought of them. What kind of craven, mean-spirited men preyed on a woman who was all by herself on a ranch, scrawled obscenities on her walls, insulted her in public? It didn't matter which of the twins she ran into. She'd seen them both try to ride off her mother's horses. They were both involved.

Just then, the cowboy collecting invitations stepped away from the door to assist a woman who was unloading a pickup.

KC looked around anxiously. It was now or never. "Come on," she told KC and Liza. With a toss of her long, dark hair, KC led them through the front door, trying to look as if she belonged there. Faith and Winnie slipped in right behind.

The thick, moist warmth inside was slightly suffocating after the crisp cold. KC inhaled the smells of hay and livestock, people and food, which all mingled into one strange heady blend.

"There must be over a hundred people here already," Faith gasped as they moved into the large, open barn which had been converted into a wonderland of Christmas decorations: lights, wreaths, holly sprigs, and Christmas balls were everywhere. Christmas carols were being piped in from speakers hidden in the high ceiling rafters.

"The more people the better," said Kimberly. "No one will notice us."

KC put her hand on Kimberly's shoulder. Of them all, Kimberly was the most apprehensive about crashing the party. Maybe it was because being black in a sea of mostly white faces made her feel even more conspicuous.

The public humiliation of being thrown out of this party wasn't something KC relished the thought of. Besides the embarrassment, it would *not* be good public relations for the ranch. She couldn't let those worries hold her back, though.

"We're not committing a crime, we're just crashing a party," KC said to Kimberly, trying to make them both feel better. "I mean, who could possibly know all the people who were really supposed to be invited?"

"I'll bet *he* does," said Liza, nodding toward a platform several yards away that was festooned with silver garlands and twinkling Christmas lights.

KC looked up and spotted a tall, elderly man with high cheekbones, a long, aristocratic nose, and dark, cold eyes. Despite his age, he stood with perfect posture, wearing a western-style black suit complete with a bolo tie. She knew at once he was Lewiston Tower.

Beside him was his blond grandson. This time KC was sure he was the same guy who had set the horses loose and insulted her mother. Beside Jake Tower was a beautiful blond woman wearing a country-style flounced skirt and a white man-tailored western shirt.

"Old Man Tower doesn't exactly look like a load of laughs," Winnie observed wryly. "Are you sure you still want to talk to him, KC?"

"Absolutely," KC resolved, steeling her nerves. "That's why I'm here."

"And *that's* why *I'm* here," Liza said, pointing to the band coming onstage behind the Towers. Each musician was dressed in a cowboy hat, western shirt, jeans, and cowboy boots. A drummer, keyboardist, and a guitarist made up the band. Then a tall young man with a bright-red mustache, in a black hat, a heavily fringed suede jacket, jeans, and lizard-skin boots, came to the microphone set up on the center of the stage. The crowd hooted in approval and settled down immediately.

"From your description, I guess that must be your pal," KC said to Liza. "He's cute."

Liza shrugged. "If you like the hillbilly type."

"Let's hang up our coats," Faith suggested. "I'm roasting in here." They found a spot off in the corner where metal racks had been set up for coats. KC hung up her jacket and smoothed her simple denim dress. She decided on the dress because she wanted to look serious and formidable when confronting old Mr. Tower. But she figured it wouldn't hurt to look a little country, too. It might make her seem less like an outsider.

Coyote Gates stepped up to the microphone. "Howdy!" he greeted the guests. "Welcome to the eleventh annual Tower barn dance. We're the Lonely Rangers, and it is our very great pleasure to play for you here tonight. So, without further ado, let's get to it!" The band began a rollicking rendition of "The Orange Blossom Special."

"Might as well get this over with," said KC as all around her couples began dancing. "Wish me luck."

"Good luck," her friends said at once.

KC weaved her way through the dancers, keeping Lewiston Tower in her sights. The old man sat on the far corner of the stage, wearing a sour expression, as though he derived no pleasure from any of the festivities. Seeing him now, KC had no difficulty believing that he was the source of all the trouble her mother was experiencing.

Thank God Grandma Rose didn't marry him, she thought, shuddering at the idea of having him for her grandfather.

Suddenly a woman spun out alongside her, knocking KC off balance. KC careened forward, flailing her arms in a vain attempt to regain her equilibrium. It was no use. The heel of her boot slipped out from under her. She was about to go down when a strong hand reached out and grabbed her arm.

KC looked up, pushing her hair out of her eyes. Her heart stopped. She was staring up into the warm, blue eyes of the rodeo rider she'd seen on the poster.

"Are you all right?" he asked. He smiled softly, and she saw he had a dimple in his right cheek.

"Yes, thank you," KC mumbled. It was definitely him, only he didn't seem like a wild rider. He was about her age, maybe a year or two older. Tall and slim, yet broad-shouldered. It seemed impossible that he was real and standing so near.

He appeared to be dazed, too, unable to take his eyes off her. "Would you like to dance?"

"Sure," KC murmured. The band had moved on to a cover of "Love in the Nick of Time." The rodeo rider took KC in his arms. Beneath his denim shirt she felt strong muscles. She inhaled his scent, a mix of clean soap and a light after-shave. His hand on her back was electric, as if it were shooting sparks of excitement right through her. They moved easily, as if they'd been dancing together for years.

Up close she saw that he wore one small jade half-moon earring, and that his hair, though cut short in front, grew in long dark waves down his back. He had a white, jagged scar on his forehead, just above his left eye.

KC shut her eyes and floated on the feeling of the rodeo rider's arms. She forgot about everything—old man Tower, her friends, the ranch. The only reality was the powerful, intoxicating, sweetness of being close to him.

Liza clapped and jumped in a circle, aware of Coyote Gates gazing down at her from the stage. The husky cowboy who had asked her to dance moved in step with her, shaking his shoulders in time to the music. It seemed that everyone in the place was dancing. No one could resist the irrepressible, high-spirited music of The Lonely Rangers. As much as Liza hated to admit it, Coyote Gates and his band were absolutely foot-stomping hot.

After about forty-five minutes, the band said they would take a short break and be right back. Liza thanked her dance partner and made a quick getaway. As she moved through the crowd, she saw KC walking by with a gorgeous cowboy who looked somehow vaguely familiar. Liza tried to recall where she'd seen him before, but she couldn't. In the next second, she was distracted by a rough tap on her shoulder.

"So, are we good enough for your little gig?" asked Coyote mockingly. Liza couldn't stand his self-satisfied smirk. But she had to admit that seeing him here, the star of this show in his flamboyant cowboy gear, she was suddenly aware that someone—maybe not her, but someone—might consider him attractive.

"What makes you think I have a *little* gig to offer?" Liza countered.

Coyote laughed. "Because it doesn't pay nothing!" he hooted.

Liza's hands flew to her hips. "That's just the kind of shortsighted hick mentality which is going to get you absolutely nowhere in the music business!" she stormed at him. "It so happens that my *little gig* is a golden chance of a lifetime. I supposed you've never heard of Mrs. Angeletti!"

" 'Fraid not."

Liza laughed haughtily. She'd show Mr. Big-Shot Cowboy who was and was not small potatoes. She could tell him anything she liked, and this local hick wouldn't know the difference. "Mrs. A. is only an internationally famous society hostess. She was featured on *Lifestyles of the Rich and Famous*," Liza lied extravagantly. "When Mrs. A. takes over a place, people from everywhere—and I mean everywhere—take notice. We're expecting Robin Leach up at the ranch any day now with a camera crew. Speaking of camera crews, did you know they filmed a major motion picture at her last place?"

"What was the name of it?" Coyote challenged.

"*U and Me,*" Liza said, naming the movie that had been filmed at the University of Springfield. "It hasn't been released yet, but it starred Alec Brady. And the band who was playing there at the time was prominently featured in the film, I might add. They landed a major recording contract."

Suddenly, with a sinking feeling, Liza realized that everyone around them was staring.

"She's going to get us kicked out of here, for sure," Winnie whispered anxiously. Faith, Kimberly, and she were hovering near the refreshment table, observing Liza's scene with Coyote Gates. Several guys had asked them to dance, but they'd quickly broken away after a few twirls on the dance floor.

"I don't believe her!" sighed Faith, rolling her eyes. "Everyone heard what Liza said about Mrs. Angeletti. She has the most unbelievably big mouth."

"Someone is bound to tell Mr. Tower. We

should get bounced out of here any second now," Kimberly agreed, looking around.

"Not to mention that she's blowing any chance of us booking the Lonely Rangers at the Lazy Q," Faith added. "And you know they would be an incredible draw. The people around here are crazy about them. I can see why. They're great. That guy I was dancing with before told me they were the most popular band in the entire area."

"I'm starting to agree with you, Faith," said Kimberly. "Maybe we should teach Liza a lesson—give her a taste of her own medicine."

"What?" Faith asked, munching on a pretzel. "Do you mean the matchmaking plan?"

"Yeah. From the way she was sparring with that Gates guy, there's bound to be something there, some attraction. And he came down from the stage to find her. We should give them a push and let Liza experience the love-hate relationship of the century," Kimberly said.

Faith's eyes brightened. "Let's do what we talked about last night," she said. "Come on."

Winnie began to follow Kimberly and Faith toward the stage, but Kimberly turned and stopped her. "Maybe you should stay here until we come back."

"Why?" Winnie asked, confused.

"You might give it away," Kimberly replied. "I don't think you have the poker face required to pull this off."

"I don't even know what you're going to do," Winnie protested.

Kimberly looked over to Faith, who was almost to the stage. "We'll be right back," she said as she ran ahead.

Winnie folded her arms angrily. *Man, make one little cooking mistake and everyone assumes you're a moron,* she fumed silently.

She ambled along the outskirts of the crowd as it moved together in a group dance. Stomp, kick, turn, clap: the barn shook. For a moment, Winnie considered joining in the fun, but her heart wasn't in it.

When she got to the entrance of the barn she stopped and watched old man Tower, still sitting up on the platform near a fake white Christmas tree decorated with blue balls. He'd been sitting there for a long time, imperiously watching the dance. Winnie didn't envy KC, having to confront him.

But Winnie didn't see a whole lot of confronting going on. All she saw was a lot of dancing with a good-looking cowboy.

A cooling breeze wafted in from the doorway. Winnie let it rush over her. It was getting hot inside the barn. With a quick glance, she saw that there was no longer anyone guarding the doorway. If she stepped outside for a second, she wouldn't have any trouble getting back in.

Winnie moved toward the door for a breath of air, but as she did, someone put a hand on her shoulder. She whirled around and faced the lovely blonde who had been standing with the Towers. Up close, she was even prettier, with large blue eyes and flawless porcelaine skin. "Can we step outside a moment?" the blonde asked anxiously. "I'd like to speak to you privately."

"Sure," said Winnie, moving out the open door.

Winnie was instantly cooled. She stood hugging herself for warmth as the wind tossed her hair.

With a quick glance over her shoulder, the woman began to speak. "I just wanted to warn you that Mr. Tower knows you and your friends have crashed the dance. Someone told him about the little dustup your girlfriend had with Coyote Gates."

"Is he mad?"

"Furious."

Winnie sighed. "Thanks for the warning, uh . . ."

"Suzanna," the young woman replied. "I'm Jake Tower's fiancée."

"My friend just came to talk to Jake's grandfather,"

Winnie explained, hoping to seize the opportunity. "You see, her mother just took over the Angel Ranch, and she's having a really hard time. She deserves a break, which she's not getting from your fiancé. If they could only talk—"

At that moment, Winnie spotted KC in the doorway, dancing in the arms of the rodeo rider. "Over there." Winnie pointed at KC. "That's KC Angeletti, and it's her mother who owns the ranch and—"

When Suzanna spotted KC, she gasped and grabbed Winnie's arms. "Does she know who she's dancing with?" Suzanna asked urgently. "That's Jeremy Tower, Jake's twin brother!"

"But they don't look a thing alike," Winnie said.

"They're not identical twins." Suzanna wrung her hands. "When Mr. Tower spots this he's going to go crazy," she wailed. "I'd better get back inside and see if I can run interference before anyone gets hurt."

"Hurt?" Winnie cried, alarmed.

"Oh, you don't know him," Suzanna said, already beginning to move away from Winnie. "He has a vicious temper. He's a mean man when he's angry." With that, she took off at a near-run, disappearing into the barn.

Wide-eyed, Winnie looked at KC. All around them, people were dancing to the fast beat of the music. But KC and the rodeo rider swayed in each other's arms.

Winnie knew she had to do something. She had to separate KC from Jeremy Tower—and fast.

Eight

aith hovered at the corner of the platform stage, wondering how she was going to maneuver herself into a position where she could put her little matchmaking scheme into motion. "I have to get closer," she said.

"This isn't going to work," Kimberly fretted. "The band won't take a break again for another forty minutes, at least." As she spoke, an unpleasant twang rang out.

Faith looked sharply to the stage and saw that Coyote had broken a guitar string. He stomped to the far side of the stage and opened his guitar case.

"This might be our chance," she told Kimberly. "You remember what to do?"

"Ready, set, go," Kimberly breathed.

Faith turned so that she was facing away from the stage. "Poor Liza." She sighed loudly, pretending to be unaware of Coyote behind her. "She's just head-over-heels about that Coyote. It was love at first sight for her. She's totally out of control over him. She told me so herself."

"A guy like that will only break her heart," Kimberly jumped in. "Liza is so passionate. And you know how she acts when she likes a guy."

"Don't I ever." Faith laughed. "When she's nuts about a guy, she antagonizes him and challenges everything he says. Those of us who know her realize it's a sure sign that she's really hooked."

"It's a shame she's going to get hurt. Coyote Gates sounds so arrogant that he'll probably never get to know the real Liza," Kimberly continued. "Only a jerk would be so nasty to such a sweet girl."

"I know," Faith agreed. "Liza is one of a kind. But someday she'll meet someone who's good enough for her."

As she spoke, Faith slowly turned her head so that she could sneak a peek at Coyote. His stunned expression told her that their little act had had its desired effect. "Oh, well," she concluded with a pained sigh, "it's his loss. Liza is better off without him. But she sure is wild about him right now."

With a small nod, she motioned for Kimberly to walk off with her. "Well?" Kimberly asked, when they were a small distance away. "Do you think our little conversation did the trick, or did we lay it on too thick?"

Faith looked back at Coyote. He was walking across the stage with a thoughtful expression on his face. He had definitely heard them. They'd have to wait to see what he chose to do about it. "Time will tell," said Faith. "Next we have to work on Liza. Where is she, anyway?"

"I don't know, but Winnie's over by the door, and she doesn't look too happy." Kimberly craned her neck to see above the crowd.

"You're right," Faith agreed, frowning. "We'd better see what's wrong."

Skirting the perimeter of the crowd, they hurried over to where Winnie stood biting her lip and shifting from foot to foot. "What's wrong, Win?" Faith asked. "You seem upset."

"We have to find KC!" Winnie said, seeming close to tears. "Something terrible has happened. She's with Jeremy Tower. One of the Tower twins!"

"You mean that cute guy she was dancing with is a Tower?" Faith gasped. "Does she know?"

"She couldn't," Winnie said. "She'd sooner spit in the Towers' eyes than dance with one of them. And Jake Tower's fiancée told me the old man will bust a gut if he sees them together."

"Well, where did she go?" Kimberly asked.

"I don't know. One minute she was right in front of me, and then I looked away for a second —to check if any bouncers had stopped you guys—and when I looked back, she was gone. I don't see her anywhere! Now the Towers are onto us, and they're going to flip when they see KC with Jeremy. Someone might get hurt and—"

"Slow down," Faith told her. "You have *no* idea where KC went?"

"None!" said Winnie. "She's disappeared with that guy!"

KC rested her head on the rodeo rider's shoulder as they swayed to the music. She knew she was supposed to be talking to old Mr. Tower, but somehow he seemed very unreal and faraway right now. The only real thing was the rodeo rider holding her in his arms. When the song ended she looked up at him and smiled. He returned her smile as they slowly drew apart. "It's awfully hot in here," he said. "Feel like taking a walk outside?"

"All right," she agreed. "Just let me get my

coat." They went to the wire racks and searched through the tightly packed coats until they dug out their own. The rodeo rider pulled on a heavy brown coat with a black leather collar while KC buttoned her gray one.

"Let's go," he said, gently steering her out the door.

"You're right, it's better out here," KC said as she and the rodeo rider walked away from the barn.

"I hate crowds," he said, jamming his hands in his pockets. "But once in a while you meet somebody interesting."

His voice was teasing yet warm. KC gazed up at his eyes, which appeared to be an even deeper blue under the evening sky. She thought of the poster and how free and wild he'd seemed. Now she saw something else as well. A touch of sadness tinged his face, even when he smiled. It was just a trace, but it was there. She had to know more about him.

"I've seen you before," she said.

He pushed up his scruffed cowboy hat. "Where?"

"On that rodeo poster in The Hungry Horse."

He chuckled softly. "That stupid thing. I don't know why they used my picture. It's kind of embarrassing. At least they didn't use the shot where I got flipped off that bronc."

"It seems incredibly dangerous."

"The danger is part of the appeal," he admitted, perching on top of the split-rail fence. "There would be no excitement to the thing if it was safe. The next step is bull riding." He laughed and shook his head. "Now there's a creature that is dead set against having anything on its back. It's the nature of the beast. I've signed up for the first bull-riding event at the Christmas rodeo. That'll be a first for me. Who knows, it might be a last, too."

"Why?" KC asked.

"Well, bull riding is a lot rougher than busting broncos. It takes less skill, but it's tougher to stay on. And if you don't get out of the ring once you're thrown, the bull will gore or stomp the living daylights out of you."

"Aren't you scared?"

"Sure." He looked away as though he were ashamed to admit it.

KC felt a powerful urge to touch him, and she put her hand on his arm. "I'd hate to see you get hurt."

"I won't get hurt. I'm indestructible," he said, smiling.

KC laughed. He was so like her in some ways. She knew she wasn't physically indestructible, but sometimes she thought she was emotionally indestructible. Time and again she was proven wrong, but she wanted to believe it nonetheless. "Nobody's indestructible," she remarked as he took hold of her hand and they walked down the road along the split-rail fence.

"I know," he said. "What I'd really like to do is run a ranch. I'd be damn good at it, too. I almost had a shot at it once, but things got screwed up."

"Things have a way of doing that," KC said sympathetically, thinking of her mother.

"Riding a bull is just the natural next step for someone as bullheaded as me." He laughed.

"I've been called bullheaded, too," KC confessed with a smile.

"I can't believe that," he said tenderly. "Not someone as beautiful as you." And then his arms were around her and his lips were on hers. She slid her hands along the back of his neck and through the soft hair that grew long there. Then somehow they turned. KC was now backed up against the fence as he kissed her. She felt the hard wood pressing against her back through her coat, but it didn't bother her.

KC didn't want the moment to end. But faraway voices floated into her consciousness. They got closer. Were there people nearby? It didn't matter. Nothing mattered but him.

"I said, let that little tramp go!" a male voice boomed.

This time there was no ignoring it. Still holding her, the rodeo rider turned. Over his shoulder, KC saw Lewiston Tower, Jake Tower and the blond woman.

"Is there a problem, Grandfather?" the rodeo rider asked.

"Grandfather!" KC gasped. She looked at him in disbelief. But he didn't look a thing like Jake Tower! She hadn't heard about another brother, but of course, there could be one. Or maybe they were fraternal twins, not identical ones. That idea had never even occured to her. With a jerk, she yanked herself away from him. "Lewiston Tower is your grandfather?"

"One hundred percent right, young lady," Lewiston Tower answered, his eyes boring into KC. "And let me tell you that gate-crashers are not welcome at my party. Your behavior is not only disrespectful and brazen, but shameful. Then again, I guess one can't expect much from someone with your family name."

KC's jaw dropped, but no words came out. She was too stunned and confused. She looked from grandfather to grandson. "Who are you?" she managed to ask.

"Jeremy Tower," the cowboy replied, his eyes searching her face. "Who are *you*?"

"Oh, this is rich!" Jake Tower sneered before KC could respond.

"Shut up, Jake," Jeremy snapped, stepping forward.

Jake laughed. "You fool! You've been here making out with one of the bitches from the Angel Ranch. She's an Angeletti."

KC watched Jeremy's strong hand curl into a fist as he lunged at his twin brother.

"Stop!" shrieked the blonde, jumping between them with her arms waving. "Stop it!"

"Get out of the way, Suzanna!" Jeremy shouted. But the woman stood her ground.

KC's head swam. How could he be a Tower— part of the family that was trying to ruin her mother? It was impossible. It couldn't be.

But it was true.

And now she was in the middle of this awful scene. So much for her clearing things up with old man Tower. She'd made everything worse. Much worse. She'd humiliated herself and her mother.

Then an even more nauseating thought hit her. If Jeremy was the other Tower twin, then he was also responsible for the things they'd done to her mother. He'd been the other rider, driving off the horses.

KC began to back away.

"There she is!" she heard Winnie shout. KC looked toward the barn and saw her friends coming out. As soon as they spotted her, they broke into a run.

"Excuse me," KC said with all the dignity she could muster. The warmth of Jeremy's kisses was still on her lips, but KC couldn't bring herself to look at him even as she stepped past him and his brother.

"I won't forget this intrusion," Lewiston Tower shouted after her. "Next time, know that you don't belong."

And I won't forget your rudeness, KC thought bitterly. But she said nothing in return. Instead, she walked with her head held high until she met up with her friends by Kimberly's van.

"What happened?" Faith asked urgently.

"I'll tell you later," KC said, terrified that the tingling at her cheekbones would turn into tears at any moment. Right now, that would be the worst possible thing to happen. "Let's just get out of here, fast?"

Nine

·····················

The next morning, Kimberly awoke and wiped away a circle of frost from her bedroom window. She smiled at the accumulation of snow before her. It had begun snowing the night before and had kept on clear through the night. Now the sky was a crisp blue and the acres of grazing fields visible from her window were a sea of white broken only by the snow-laden pines.

She roused Faith and insisted they go out to test the area for the best sledding runs. Kimberly was eager to contribute her services as a professional "winter adventure guide." Now that the snow was here, maybe guests would start to arrive. She was determined to be fully prepared when they did.

After grabbing a quick breakfast in the silent kitchen, she and Faith bundled up and trudged out into the snow, dragging their sleds behind them.

"Look out!" Kimberly shouted, as she watched Faith zoom down a hillside on one of the newly revamped American Flyers. But Faith didn't seem to hear her—or to notice the pine she was quickly approaching. Kimberly covered her eyes, cringing at the crash that was sure to follow.

A moment passed and no crash or cry came. When she peeked out from between her gloved fingers, Kimberly saw Faith shift her weight and neatly swerve around the tree. "Way to go," she cheered, punching her fist in the air. She ran off to meet Faith, who was slowing to a stop at the bottom of the hill. "I thought you were about to crack your head on that tree," she said.

"A sledding ace like me? No way!" Faith laughed. "But I would classify that hill as advanced —no little kids or geeks allowed."

Kimberly pulled a pad from the deep side pocket of her down jacket and flipped it open. On the first page she'd drawn a map of the field immediately to the left of the stable. *Advanced hill about fifteen yards from corral fence,* she wrote about the downhill run Faith had just tested. "Any boulders or weird curves?" she asked Faith.

"No, but there's a sudden drop that gives you a good jolt and could wipe you out if you were a beginner. Plus, there's that pine tree."

Kimberly sketched in the tree and wrote, *sudden drop*, on her pad. "Duly noted," she said, grinning. "Every trail expertly marked. How much more professional can you get?"

"Not much," said Faith. As they spoke, a flurry of snow started up again. "Keep it up!" Faith yelled to the skies. "We want more snow! Lots of it!"

"Maybe this will cheer KC up," Kimberly said hopefully.

"I don't think anything could do that," said Faith. "She was so shook up last night. You saw how pale she was. She barely even spoke. It was like she was physically sick over what happened. I felt really bad for her."

"It's a western Romeo and Juliet," Kimberly said, shaking her head sadly.

"I hope not. You know what happened to them."

"Yeah, I guess that romance didn't turn out too well," said Kimberly. "I wonder if KC will ever see Jeremy Tower again."

"Not to hear her tell it," Faith said as she stood and brushed snow from her hair. "She says she never wants to lay eyes on him again. Of course, she's lying, but it *is* the sensible approach."

"It's hard to be sensible when it comes to love —or attraction, or infatuation, or whatever on earth it is," Kimberly observed.

"If anyone can talk herself into doing the sensible thing, it's KC," Faith said. "Most of the time, anyway. But, you know, I've never seen her like this. She really adored Peter, but even with him she wasn't all moony and lovestruck. This Tower guy really got under her skin in a short time—and in a big way."

"I could see that," Kimberly agreed.

"Want to hear something really bent?" Faith asked as they began to walk across the snow-covered field, pulling their sleds behind them.

Kimberly smiled. "Of course."

"Even though KC's romance has made her completely, abjectly miserable, it's made *me* want to have a Christmas romance. You know, someone to kiss under the mistletoe and go all goofy over."

"I thought you wanted a break from guys," Kimberly reminded her.

"That's what I thought, but maybe I only needed a short break, because I'm ready to get all hot and bothered over some idiot again."

"Not me," shouted Kimberly, breaking into a joyful run. "All I want is to find the perfect sledding slope for the ultimate, professionally guided sledding adventure." She stopped and scooped up enough snow for a snowball. Packing it quickly, she hurled it at Faith.

Faith responded with her own snowball. Soon they were exchanging a rapid-fire volley of snowballs, ducking and laughing as they threw.

"Enough! Enough!" Kimberly panted after a while. "We have to save our strength for our next sledding adventure. And I think I see it, right there."

She led them a small distance to the base of another long run that split a cluster of snow-covered pines. "I'll do this one," Kimberly volunteered, starting to trek up the hill, dragging her sled.

The morning quickly passed into early afternoon as Kimberly and Faith continued to scope out the sledding potential of each slope on the sprawling expanse of the Angel Dude Ranch. "God! I'm soaked," Faith complained, holding up her wet arms as evidence. She gazed up at the sky, which had continued to drop fat white flakes on them. "I think we're a long way from the lodge. We'd better start getting back."

Kimberly nodded, realizing that she was becoming chilled and that the snow was falling more heavily. "Let's cut up to the road," she suggested.

"It's probably plowed by now and we won't have to trudge through all the snow."

"Good idea," Faith agreed.

When they reached the road, they realized they were almost to the front gate of the Tower Ranch. "Gosh, I didn't think we had walked *this* far!" Kimberly exclaimed, a chill running through her. She suddenly realized that her legs ached from all the walking they'd done.

"Me neither," said Faith. "Angel Ranch is at least two miles from here, maybe more."

"We might be better cutting back across the field," Kimberly said with a resigned sigh. The very thought made her shoulders sag with fatigue. Her clothing felt heavy and damp. She didn't realize she'd gotten so wet. "Right now I wish I had one of those *Star Trek* communicators and I could call someone to beam me home."

A broad smile formed on Faith's face as she looked down the road. "Guess what! Your wish has just been granted," she said.

Kimberly turned and saw a cream-colored Chevette chugging down the road toward them, wisps of steam escaping from under its front hood. It was Casper's Rent-A-Wreck. "Not exactly the *Enterprise*, but it'll do," she said happily.

Casper slowed to a stop when he saw them.

"Would you like a lift?" he asked, rolling down the window.

"Absolutely, positively," said Kimberly. "We'll have to put the sleds in the trunk." Casper shut off the engine and got out to help them.

When the sleds were loaded, Casper held the car door open. "Climb on in," he said to Faith, pushing up the front seat so she could climb into the back. He smiled and turned to Kimberly. "Your winged chariot awaits you, Wonder Woman."

"Wings are just what this jalopy could use." Kimberly laughed as she climbed in beside him. With a shiver, she pulled off her wet gloves and blew on her fingers. "Does this crate have heat?"

"That's one thing it does have," Casper said. "In fact, I had to roll down the windows on my way into town. It blasts like a furnace."

"Then let it blast," said Faith. "My toes are getting numb."

Casper turned the key in the ignition, only to have the car sputter feebly. "Uh-oh," he moaned.

Kimberly slumped into the seat. As she did, a spring jabbed her back through the worn upholstery. "Did you put antifreeze in, like I told you?" Kimberly asked.

"I did that this morning," he replied. He tried the ignition again. This time it clicked and died.

"You don't want to flood it, so don't turn it

again until I tell you," Kimberly instructed. "You wouldn't by any chance have any tools, would you?"

Grimly, Casper shook his head. Somehow Kimberly wasn't surprised.

"Hey, I know," Faith chirped with a maniacal optimism. "Why don't we just trot on up to the Tower Ranch and ask them for a wrench?"

"And hope they don't shoot us on sight," Kimberly said with a doleful smile. "Casper, turn on your lights, okay?" she told him, then she slid out of her seat and went to the front of the car. The lights weren't on.

"It's your battery this time," she called to him as she lifted the hood. On a hunch, she picked up a large rock off the side of the road and firmly rapped each of the battery's diodes. "Try it now," she yelled to Casper.

The engine coughed and then came to life. "You're a genius!" Casper cried when she climbed back into her seat beside him.

"Think so? Thanks. I saw a cousin of mine do that once on an old jalopy of his," she said. "You have so much corrosion and gunk on that battery that it's not making the connections. I just banged some of the rot away. We're lucky it worked. I suggest you get a new battery—or at least keep a rock with you at all times."

"It would be better if I could keep you with me at all times," Casper said.

Something in his voice made her look at him sharply. Was she imagining it, or was he interested in her?

No, she told herself. He didn't mean anything by it. If anyone, Kimberly would have matched Casper with Faith. Maybe he might fit the bill for Faith's Christmas romance. Besides, with his waspy, prep-school ways, Casper wasn't her type. Not to mention the black/white difference between them.

Still, Kimberly was suddenly seeing Casper in a different light. He was very sweet, and not bad-looking at all, even if he wasn't Mr. Macho. "What were you doing in town?" she asked him.

"I drove down to the liquor store and looked around to see what they had. I found one good vintage, so I ordered two cases of it for the big dinner."

"I hope it wasn't too expensive," Faith fretted.

"It was in the price range Mrs. Angeletti gave me."

Kimberly scrutinized Casper's refined, boyish face. "Are you old enough to buy alcohol?" she asked doubtfully.

"Twenty-one last week," he said with a hint of pride.

"You look younger," Faith observed bluntly.

"It's my youthful exuberance," he said wryly.

When they stepped into the front door of the lodge, the first sight they saw made them all gasp. The eight-foot Christmas tree had been set up in the lobby. "I didn't realize it was so tall," said Casper, circling the unadorned tree.

"It's so . . . so . . . perfect," Faith said. "It almost looks fake."

"Wait till it's decorated," added Kimberly. "It'll be a knockout."

"I wonder where everyone is?" Faith mused. The lodge was completely quiet.

"Probably all busy with their projects," Kimberly speculated. "I guess we've missed lunch."

"What I want is to get these wet clothes off and step into a warm shower," Faith said as she hurried upstairs.

Kimberly peeled off her jacket and hung it on a hook by the front door. When she turned back, Casper was gone. *Probably scurried upstairs to get back to work on that paper of his,* she figured. So she picked up a magazine and began to flip through it, knowing she would have to wait for Faith to get out of the shower before it would be her turn.

Casper appeared suddenly at the dining-room door. "Come and get it!" he called to her.

Kimberly looked at him. "Get what?"

"Lunch," he said. "I made us lunch."

"Well, all right," said Kimberly, moving into the dining room. The first thing she noticed was that the wide stone fireplace against the wall was ablaze with a roaring fire. "Did you light that?" she asked Casper.

"Built the fire myself," he said, leading her to a table near the fireplace. "Just because I'm not the great outdoorsman doesn't mean I'm a total dork." He pulled out a chair for her. "Please be seated, madame, your lunch is about to arrive."

"Merci, monsieur," Kimberly said, smiling.

Casper disappeared into the kitchen and reappeared a moment later, holding a tray. "Ze bacon-and-cheese omelette wis ze toasted sourdough bread is for ze beautiful lady," he said playfully as he put a fat, fragrant omelette before her. "And ze gentleman gets . . . the exact same thing."

"This is wonderful," said Kimberly after she had taken the first bite. "Where did you get this bread? It's so fresh and delicious."

"I baked it this morning," he said, handing her a cup of steaming cocoa.

"Very funny." What a strange guy he was—so accomplished and worldly in some ways, and then so kidlike in others. She knew he hadn't baked the bread, but it wouldn't have been a total surprise if he had.

Casper smiled at her. "I picked the bread up in town, and this cheese, too. I wanted a few things to munch on, since there isn't exactly room service around here. The rest of the stuff I found in the kitchen."

"You're a great omelette-maker," Kimberly said sincerely.

He smiled at the compliment. Kimberly decided he had a good smile, open and real. "I also make a mean *coq au vin*," he said.

"I believe you," said Kimberly. She looked into his lively green eyes behind his glasses and suddenly felt very comfortable with him. "Casper, why did you come all the way out here by yourself? Wouldn't you rather spend the holiday with your family?"

"I came to work, like I told you," he replied. "But I'm also interested in the hotel and guest-house business. I wanted to decide over this break if that's what I really want to do, because when I go back it will influence what courses I take. I have to start applying to grad schools to study restaurant management."

"Cornell has a good program for that," Kimberly told him, remembering a classmate who had transferred there for that exact reason. "What's your major now?"

"Journalism," he answered. "That's why I'm

doing this paper on Montana. It's a final-project kind of thing."

"You've been working hard on it," she said. "You spend most of your time in your room."

He laughed. "Thank God for laptop computers. If I was working on an old-fashioned typewriter I'd be keeping everyone awake at night with the clattering."

"No one would even hear you," said Kimberly. "We've all been working so hard that we sleep like rocks. Now, with this big dinner coming up, things are getting even more intense."

"Do you think it would be weird if I offered to wait on tables at the dinner? I've waited before, and I wouldn't expect to be paid or anything. It's just that Mrs. Angeletti is such a nice woman, I'd like to do something to help her."

"That is so sweet! It's not weird at all," Kimberly assured him. "We could sure use the help."

"There would be one condition, though," said Casper slyly. "That I get to go on at least one winter adventure with the appointed guide."

"It's a deal," Kimberly agreed, not sure whether she had just agreed to go on a date.

Just then Liza stepped into the dining room, dressed in a long, nubby yellow sweater and yellow-green leggings. Instantly, Kimberly tensed.

She didn't like the smug, knowing look Liza wore.

"Isn't this romantic," Liza boomed, just as Kimberly had feared. "A fire and everything!"

"Hello, Liza," said Kimberly without enthusiasm. With a pang of guilt, Kimberly recalled how she and Faith had sown the seeds of a romance between Liza and Coyote the day before. But as she saw Liza advancing on them like some bird of prey zeroing in on its target, her guilt dissipated. She had a feeling she was in for the legendary Liza Ruff butt-in treatment—the kind of behavior that had driven Faith to want to pay her back in kind with Coyote.

"We were just discussing my upcoming winter adventure, now that the snow has arrived," Casper told her.

A suggestive leer came across Liza's face. "Oh, you're taking Casper out on an adventure, are you? My, how exciting."

"I'm sure we'll have fun," said Kimberly, ignoring Liza's insinuation.

"I'm sure you will, too," Liza teased with a smirk. "No matter how cold it gets, you can keep each other warm."

A tinge of embarrassed blush colored Casper's temples. "Ignore her, Casper," Kimberly said. "Would you like to go skiing tomorrow?"

"I've only tried it once before," he admitted.

"Don't worry, you'll be in my hands," Kimberly said. The leer on Liza's face made Kimberly instantly wish she'd chosen other words. She glared at Liza, defying her to make a crack.

Liza threw up her arms mockingly. "You said it, Kimberly. Not me. I didn't open my mouth."

Ten

"**R**emember, if the Lonely Rangers are playing here, we're leaving," Liza stated firmly as they walked through the front door of The Hungry Horse that evening. They had just come from the early show of *The Last Ride*. In part, they were there simply to catch a burger after the movie, but Liza had a more serious agenda. So far, no one had responded to her posters. It was time for her to get out and recruit *new* talent.

"We know! You've told us that ten times already," said Faith, pulling off her furry red wool hat. "That's why Kimberly and I are here with you, to give our opinion about new talent."

"The Lonely Rangers were great, though," Kimberly reminded Liza. "They'd pack the place."

"They weren't *so* hot," Liza sniffed. "Besides, we need a group who'll work for tips, and Mr. Annoying Gates made it perfectly clear that he wouldn't consider it."

"Too bad," sighed Faith.

"Too bad for the Lonely Strange-os, you mean," Liza insisted. She bustled up to the entrance of the dining room. It was suppertime and the place was packed. "A table for three, please," she requested of a middle-aged man in a western shirt and jeans.

He grabbed three menus and showed them to a small table in the back of the crowded room. "By the way," Liza asked him as they took their seats, "what bands are playing tonight?"

With a quick smile, the man tapped the hand-printed list tacked onto the wall behind them. "Music starts at nine," he told them.

"Well, there's the good news and the bad news," Liza said as they read the list. Two bands were listed. Playing first was a group called the Razzle Dazzlers. Second was the Lonely Rangers.

"That'll work out," said Kimberly. "We'll eat, hear the Razzle Dazzlers, and then leave."

Liza nudged Kimberly. "Can't wait to get back to Casper, can you?" she teased.

"Just because I was having lunch with Casper doesn't mean we're having some wild affair. And poor Casper! You made him turn red today."

"Oh, come on," Liza scoffed. "You two looked very cozy there. Don't pretend nothing's going on."

"Nothing *is* going on, or is going to go on," Kimberly insisted.

"Why not?" Faith countered. "Casper's cute. A little geeky, but in an adorable sort of way."

"He's also white," said Kimberly.

"Would you let that stop you?" Liza shrieked. "Get with it! This is the last of the twentieth century! Modern times!"

"It probably wouldn't stop me," Kimberly said thoughtfully. "But it might stop him."

"Not our Casper. No way!" Liza said. "He's a Renaissance man, a contemporary thinker. I can tell."

"Our Casper?" Faith repeated incredulously. "Since when is he *our Casper*? KC told me you had decided he was an ax murderer!"

"A tiny error in judgment on my part," Liza said with a shrug. "I can be wrong on occasion. We're still alive, after all?"

"We certainly are," said Kimberly.

"I wish KC had come out with us tonight," said Faith as she surveyed the room of happy, laughing people. "She could use a lift. But I think she was nervous about running into Jeremy Tower."

"Winnie should have come, too," said Kimberly. "She's been so mopey since the other day."

"I'll bet she misses Josh," Faith said, getting up. "I'm going to go call them. Even though they think they want to stay in, it would do them both good to get down here and be around people."

"Yeah, look how wonderful it was the last time we were in a crowd," Liza quipped, recalling the scene outside the barn dance.

"This is different," Faith insisted. "This time we have as much right to be here as anyone else." She grabbed her purse and squeezed out of the small space between their table and the next. "I'll be right back."

"I couldn't believe KC was all over a guy she'd never even met before. And right where everyone could see her," Liza gossiped when Faith was gone.

"KC wasn't all over him," Kimberly objected.

"You know what I mean," said Liza. Why was everyone so touchy? Sometimes she felt like she couldn't say *anything* right. "Don't get me wrong, I think what she did was totally cool. I'm no puritan. Besides, that guy was beyond gorgeous! It just doesn't fit my image of her. You know, I think of her as an ice-queen type."

"I know what you're saying," Kimberly had to admit. "Sometimes she seems more pulled-together than anyone could possibly be. At least anyone our age."

"What can I get you gals?" asked a young waiter.

"We haven't even looked yet," Liza said, shooshing him away with her hand. "Come back in three minutes." She buried her head in her menu. "I'm sure this isn't as yummy as Casper's homemade cuisine," she needled Kimberly, "but I'm starving."

Liza was agonizing over the choice between a burger or a steak sandwich when she sensed someone standing beside her. "It hasn't been three minutes yet," she said without lifting her head. "We're not ready for you."

"Few people ever are," replied a familiar western voice.

Slowly, Liza lowered her menu and looked up. Coyote stood smiling down at her. "Oh, it's you. What do you want?"

"A truce," he said.

Liza eyed him skeptically. "You mean you want the Angel Ranch gig? I knew you'd change your mind."

"No, that's not it," he said, pulling a chair to their table and straddling it backward. "I simply want to be friendly. I'm really a friendly kind of guy, if you give me a chance." He extended his wide hand to Kimberly. "I'm Billy Gates. My friends call me Coyote," he introduced himself.

"Pleased to meet you," said Kimberly, shaking his hand.

"And I'm pleased to meet any friend of this young lady's." He turned and smiled at Liza. "Whose name I haven't even learned."

"And probably never will. What's going on?" Liza asked.

"I just came in a little early to check the sound system for our show later."

"Well, I'm here to audition the Razzle Dazzlers," Liza huffed.

Coyote grinned in a way that Liza found maddening and charming all at once. "They're okay for the over-fifty set, I guess."

"Thanks for your input," Liza said dryly.

"Here's some more input for you," he went on. "You know, Montana is becoming real popular with Hollywood types. People around here have mixed feelings about that. On the one hand, they don't want to get overrun with fancy types, but on the other hand, they're like everybody else, curious about movie stars. If you could get a couple of movie stars to stay at your ranch, the people would pour in just to see them."

"How would we get movie stars to come?" Kimberly asked, laughing lightly.

"I suppose I could make a few phone calls," Liza cut in quickly, not wanting Kimberly to make her look foolish by exposing her lies.

"You did tell me you knew lots of famous people, didn't you?" Coyote questioned.

"Of course," Liza replied. "But I can't just order them to drop everything and take a vacation. And what makes you think we need business, anyway?"

"Everybody knows everybody's business around here," he said matter-of-factly. "There's a lot of land but not a whole lot of people. Word gets around."

The waiter came back, but they told him they wanted to wait for Faith to return. "Let me go see what's taking her so long," said Kimberly, getting up from her seat.

With Kimberly gone, Liza looked at Coyote but said nothing. An awkward silence ensued. Liza wasn't used to silent spaces in conversation, because she was usually the one to fill them. But suddenly she felt nervous and a little shy. Coyote really *was* quite good-looking when he wasn't being obnoxious, she decided.

"Are you going to the Winter Carnival next Saturday?" he asked.

"Maybe," she replied, not wanting to tell him about being on the cleanup committee. She still couldn't believe KC had signed them up for that without even asking.

"Well, how are you at making snowmen?"

"Snowmen are my specialty," she boasted, letting her guard down a bit. "Back in Brooklyn, which is where I'm from, people would come from all the blocks around to see the snowmen I made in our front courtyard, I always made them look like someone in the neighborhood. My parents complained that it embarrassed them, but I did it anyway. When you have a talent, it's wrong not to use it, right?"

"Right." Billy smiled. "It looks like I came to the right place, then. I need a partner for the snowman-building contest at the Winter Carnival. How about it?"

"How about what?"

"Being my partner."

"Me?" *But you don't even like me!* Liza thought.

"Yes, you. Do you want to?" he pressed.

"Sure," Liza agreed quietly. "That might be fun."

"Oh, it's a blast!" Coyote assured her. "Winter Carnival is the best thing around here. You came at a good time." He lifted himself from his chair and stood smiling at her a moment. "I'll pick you up at the ranch that morning, around nine thirty. Can you be ready by then?"

"I guess," Liza said, feeling a little stunned.

"Terrific. I'll see you then. Are you staying for our show?"

"I . . . um . . . I'm not sure," she stammered. "It depends on what Faith and Kimberly want to do."

"Don't stay," he told her.

"Why not?"

"I wouldn't want to see you dancing with any other guy but me."

"You wouldn't?" she blurted, flabbergasted. This was flattering but very bizarre. "Um, can I ask you something?" she said, trying to recover.

"Sure."

"You don't have a psychiatric medical record or anything, do you? I mean, have you been known to have a split personality at times?"

"I have been known to howl at the moon from time to time," he said with a smile. "But split personality, no. No one has ever accused me of that."

"Then how come you're being so damn nice all of a sudden?" she asked bluntly.

"I've been nice all along," he insisted devilishly. "You just didn't notice. Maybe you're the one who's had a change of heart. See you on Saturday."

With a quick wave, he turned and left the dining room. Liza sat, trying to absorb the impact of his words. How had raw animosity turned into a romance? Did she want a romance—with him? It *was* flattering, of course, there was no denying that but still . . .

Several moments later, Kimberly and Faith swooped down on her. "So?" Faith asked eagerly. "What was that all about?"

"Where did you guys disappear to?" Liza asked.

"We wanted to give you time *alone*," Kimberly explained.

"Why?" Liza grumbled. "That was totally unnecessary."

"Oh, really?" Kimberly said. "It's clear that Coyote's got a thing for you."

"To tell you the truth," Faith lied, "he met Casper in the liquor store this morning. He heard Casper tell the salesman that he was shopping for the Angel Ranch, and so Coyote struck up a conversation with him. Casper said that all he did was ask about you. Casper got the impression that he was really super-interested in you."

"I don't know whether to be happy or sad over that," Liza admitted. "He *is* conceited and obnoxious, but he has a certain . . . I don't know . . . sex appeal."

"Oh, he's loaded with sex appeal," said Kimberly. "I've heard that the girls around here are all in love with him. He's a local celebrity."

"I guess it's not surprising."

"I bet he'll be a big star someday," added Faith. "He has that quality about him."

"Do you think so?" asked Liza.

"Absolutely," said Kimberly.

The waiter returned and took their orders. As Liza ate, a fantasy formed in her head. She imagined a picture of herself and Coyote together on the cover of *People*. "Yes, we met before either of us was famous," she fantasized telling an interviewer. "But the moment we met, there was an incredible chemistry, and we've been together ever since."

Was there incredible chemistry between them? she wondered. For the first time since she'd met him, Liza admitted to herself that, whether it was love or hate, there was *something* drawing them together.

"What are you thinking about?" Faith interrupted Liza's thoughts. "You're sitting there chewing and grinning like the Cheshire Cat."

In truth, Liza was still pondering the question of why Coyote had changed so much, but she didn't feel like discussing it. "Snowmen," Liza answered. "I was thinking about snowmen."

Eleven

"Now maybe everything will change," said KC hopefully.

"Keep up the good work, snow!" Faith cried to the morning sky, which was once again spilling snowflakes on them. At the sound of her cheer the horse beside her whinnied and backed up two steps. "Are you sure you want to do this?" Faith asked KC. "I don't know if riding into town is such great idea. That banker would understand if you called and canceled your mom's appointment. The bank might even be closed on account of the snow."

"They're not. I called to confirm the appointment," KC assured her. "This is really no problem. I've ridden before."

"Twice," Faith reminded her. "That doesn't exactly make you a pro."

"I'm just going to trot into town. I'm not missing this appointment with my mother's banker just because the roads aren't plowed yet," KC insisted. "It's too important."

"I picked Mountaingirl for you because she's pretty gentle," said Faith, stroking the brown and white horse. "I had her out on the road the other day, and cars don't seem to spook her at all."

Just then, Mrs. Angeletti came hurrying through the knee-deep snow. "KC, I found some more papers you might need," she said, pulling several documents from under her coat. "Oh, you shouldn't be doing this," she fretted. "I should go. Let me call Ms. Cartlyn and postpone the appointment."

"No. Your first loan payment is due in two days, Mom," KC reminded her mother again. "You don't want to go in there having missed a payment already. It's not good psychologically."

"How did you get so smart?" Mrs. Angeletti asked with a note of pride.

"Your tuition dollars at work," KC replied lightly. "Now, what are these papers?"

Mrs. Angeletti quickly explained the documents.

"Ms. Cartlyn is very easy to talk to," she said as KC folded the papers into the leather pouch at her waist. "I really appreciate this. And be careful on that horse, please."

KC climbed into the saddle and picked up the reins. "We'll be fine, won't we, Mountaingirl," KC addressed the horse.

"Good luck," Faith called as KC set out from the ranch. Through the falling snow, Mountaingirl kept up a steady gait. KC and the horse soon fell into an easy rhythm.

As she passed the front gate and went out into the road, KC felt as if she were in a fairy tale. The snow on the ground was completely unmarked by tracks. It lay like a shimmering blanket, covering everything.

For the first time since the barn dance, KC felt at peace. In this magical setting, what did cowboys, old cattle barons, or anything else matter? She half expected a red-coated gnome to step out of the snow-covered woods and offer to grant her three wishes.

What would she wish for? she wondered, letting her mind wander. *That Dad was alive* was the first thought that sprang to her mind. *And that the ranch would be a big, super success.*

KC came to the main road leading into town. It had been plowed, but the snow was busily recovering it with white. Few cars passed because of the early hour and the weather. KC was glad. They didn't disturb Mountaingirl, but they did make KC very nervous. The people around here all seemed to drive big vehicles—pickups, vans, jeeps. And they drove them fast. KC didn't want to have to deal with them blowing her off the road, or skidding into her on the snow.

After almost half an hour, KC was nearly to downtown Towerton. Just outside of town, she trotted past the rodeo arena, a large, domed building on a flat tract of land. Peering through the lightly falling snow, KC saw the solitary figure of a cowboy walking a black stallion, only several yards from the road.

With a jolt, KC realized the cowboy was Jeremy.

Her heart slammed into her chest as she struggled to keep calm. Despite all the heady urging of her senses, the facts told a different story. The facts clearly stated that Jeremy had done cruel things to her mother. She could never forgive him. She had to accept that he was a Tower—and could never be her dream man.

As if he'd heard her thoughts, Jeremy looked up.

KC clapped her heels against the horse's sides. "Go, Mountaingirl," she cried, sitting forward and letting out the reins. Mountaingirl heeded the signal and took off at a gallop. KC leaned forward, gripping the reins, terrified, yet determined to get away.

Even with her head start, Jeremy was soon right behind her on the stallion. "Stop! Please!" he shouted. "Stop!"

His voice spurred her on to ride even harder, widening the gap between them. Her heart pounded and every muscle in her body was coiled with tension, but still she rode. She felt as if her very life depended on getting away.

The downtown area soon came into view. It was insanity to ride a horse at full speed through the streets, but she couldn't slow down. If she did, she'd have to talk to him—see him, hear him, drink in his presence.

"Go, Mountaingirl! Go!" KC urged the horse. Jeremy was now nearly even with her. She kept her eyes straight, not daring to look at him. But the next thing she knew, he was in front of her—and blocking her path.

A scream uncoiled from deep inside KC as Mountaingirl reared back onto two legs. Below her, the earth spun wildly.

KC clutched Mountaingirl's mane, but still she felt herself slipping.

Suddenly Jeremy leapt from his horse and onto Mountaingirl's back. "Whoa there, steady, easy does it," he soothed the horse firmly as he grabbed the reins from behind KC. His warmth surrounded her as he brought the horse down onto all fours. "Are you okay?" he asked.

KC trembled uncontrollably. She wanted desperately to stop, but her body wouldn't. Despite the snow, her forehead was damp with sweat. She didn't know whether to thank him for saving her or scream at him for cutting her off.

She realized that since the dance he'd taken on a dreamlike quality in her head, but now he was right next to her, very real. She turned and looked up at his deep blue eyes. Yes, he was real, all right. The scar, the earring, the wavy dark hair that grew long in back—she took it all in. He was as real and as attractive as he'd been at the dance.

He got off Mountaingirl and back on his own horse. "Why did you run away without talking to me?" he asked, bringing his horse alongside her.

"How can you ask me that, after everything you've done? How can you even speak to me?"

"What have I done?"

"You know very well! Setting the horses free! Writing that filth on the stable! How could you do those things? I hate you for it. I hate you!"

Behind them, a pickup stopped, unable to pass. "Hey, move those animals!" the driver cried.

"We can hitch the horses over there at that post at the park," Jeremy said.

Not knowing what else to do, KC dismounted and walked her horse over to the post. Wordlessly, Jeremy hitched his horse and then reknotted KC's rope. While he did so, KC began to walk away.

She got only a few feet when his strong hand was on her shoulder. "Listen to me," he began. "I have no idea what you're talking about, but I was in school until last Saturday. I got home the morning of the dance. So anything you think I did, I couldn't possibly have done. I wasn't here."

"You were in school?" KC asked dubiously. "What school?"

"Bozman. I'm studying ranch management."

KC peered into his eyes, searching for the truth behind his words. He was being honest, all her instincts told her that. Still, she didn't want to let down her guard. "I know your brother was involved," she said. "Did he tell you what's been going on?"

"I don't talk to my brother much. I got the idea that there's no love lost between our families, but I didn't know they had done anything to hurt your mother."

"They're trying to run my mother out of business," KC said, hearing the anger fading from her voice. She couldn't let that happen. Her anger was her only defense. "They . . . you . . . someone . . . let her horses out of the stable. They wrote obscenities and warnings on her barn, they're bad-mouthing her in town. Your brother insulted her right to her face."

"Why?"

"I don't know. Your brother implied that everyone around here hates outsiders. But no one else has bothered us. Just your brother and . . . and . . . you."

"Not me," he said gently.

"Well, I saw someone else with him the day he let the horses run loose."

"It wasn't me," Jeremy repeated.

It was happening again, the same feeling she'd had at the barn dance when she first gazed into his dark-blue eyes. It was what she imagined drowning might be like, once you realized nothing could save you. Giving up. Going under.

She felt his strong hand on her back, and then his lips on hers. She held him close and closed her eyes, kissing him back.

A loud "ahem" suddenly made KC pull away. It was Jake's fiancée. She was standing there, facing them with a scowl on her pretty, delicate face.

"Jeremy, when are you going to learn to leave well enough alone?" she asked mildly.

"Good morning, Suzanna. Nice to see you, too," Jeremy taunted her, holding on to KC's arm. "And you're right. I never did learn how to tow the old man's line, like the rest of the Towers."

"Your grandfather has been very good to all of us," Suzanna said. "Why can't you appreciate all he's done for you?"

Jeremy smiled at her coldly. "Very good. You'll fit into the family just fine. As long as you're on Grandfather's side, you win. So you tell yourself he's right—no matter what despicable thing he does."

"You're a fool, Jeremy. A self-destructive fool," Suzanna replied, her voice growing heated with frustration.

"Maybe so, but I'll never be his toady, like my butt-kissing brother."

"Jake loves Grandfather," Suzanna cried.

"It's Grandfather's money and power he loves. And so do you. Nobody could really love that old tyrant. Oh, yeah, you'll fit into the family without any trouble. You might as well change your name from Cartlyn to Tower right now. Then everyone will know you're one of the big, bad, all-powerful Tower family. I know you can't wait."

"That's unfair, Jeremy," Suzanna insisted. "Unfair and untrue. I think you know that."

Cartlyn! KC sucked in her breath at the sound of the name. Could Suzanna be *the* Ms. Cartlyn, the banker? Surely not. *Oh, please, not!* KC prayed.

"Jeremy, I have to go," KC said, pulling away. "I'm almost late for a very important appointment at the bank."

"So am I," said Suzanna. "With Ms. Angeletti here."

Jeremy let go of KC's arm and stepped toward Suzanna. "You do what KC asks," he said. "That's the least our family can do to make up for what's happened."

"This is banking business," Suzanna said, tossing back her blond hair defiantly. "It has nothing to do with family."

"I have to go," KC said, pulling away from him.

"We'll meet up again." He looked deep into KC's eyes. "That's for certain." Then he jumped up onto his horse and rode quickly away.

"I'm sorry for that scene," Suzanna apologized. "But you really don't know what you're getting yourself into."

KC's head was spinning. She was speechless. So many strong emotions were running through her at once: embarrassment, anger, infatuation. Or was it love? The strongest thing she felt was the urge to run away.

She couldn't, though. Her mother was counting on her.

"I hope you won't hold this against me." KC forced herself to speak in a controlled voice.

"Come inside," Suzanna said. "It's cold. The bank is just across the street. In fact, I could see the commotion with the horses from my office window. That's why I came out."

KC followed Suzanna into the small, quiet bank. "Right in here," Suzanna said, holding open a door with her name lettered on it. She sat behind her desk and looked at KC levelly. "Before we get on to business, let me tell you a few things about Jeremy."

"Sure," said KC. Beautiful Suzanna—with her blunt, cut blond hair and stylish blue suit—couldn't have been more than five years older than she, yet, beside her KC suddenly felt very young. Suzanna had the polished, professional image KC hoped to cultivate herself someday. Everything about Suzanna was meticulous: her buffed nails, her understated makeup, her poise. She was confident and accomplished. Still in her twenties, she had her own office. The way she'd stood up to Jeremy was impressive, too. The other day she hadn't hesitated to jump in between the fighting brothers, and just now she hadn't let Jeremy intimidate her. KC decided that Suzanna was someone she could admire.

That was all the more reason KC didn't really want to hear what Suzanna was about to say.

"Jeremy is a mess. He's the black sheep of the family," Suzanna said with the authority and charm of a TV anchorwoman. "Actually, he's one of two black sheeps. The other is his father, who ran off to Alaska to work on the pipeline and never came back."

"What makes Jeremy a black sheep?" KC dared to ask.

"It's no one thing," said Suzanna. "But it's everything he does. Like riding in the rodeo, for example. I know he does that just to worry his grandfather to death."

"But he's studying ranching," KC reminded her.

Suzanna shuffled some papers on her desk. "Well, I suppose if he studies *and* cools down, maybe someday he'll be ready to take over. I can't see that happening, though. He isn't ready. He'd sink the ranch within a year. But why worry? More likely he'll stick with the rodeo until some bull kicks him in the head one day."

KC flinched at the thought. She needed to change the subject quickly. "Let me tell you why I'm here, Ms. Cartlyn."

"Suzanna."

"All right," KC said with a small smile. "My mother needs an extension on her first loan date. And she could use another loan." KC tried to gauge Suzanna's reaction, but the woman just listened intently, keeping a neutral expression. "A small loan would see her through this opening season." KC began speaking rapidly. "Angel Dude Ranch is a sound investment—a sure success. It's only that renovations have been costly, and as you know, the weather has just now changed. We have very big plans for the ranch, but things haven't gotten off the ground quite as quickly as expected. We need a little more time."

"To be honest," said Suzanna, "I told your mother that she wasn't asking for enough money in her initial loan. I'm not surprised she's having difficulty now. She should have taken more money right from the start. But she's new to the business, and people always underestimate start-up costs on new ventures. There are so many hidden expenses no one anticipates."

"That's exactly what happened," KC said, relieved that Suzanna understood. "Is there any way you can extend her more money? About ten thousand?"

Suzanna leaned forward and clasped her hands together. "Quite frankly, I don't know. Having issued her first loan, I'm well aware of your mother's financial situation. Right now, she's not what the bank would consider a good risk. I really had to go to bat for her in order to get the first loan."

KC didn't like the sound of this. "Could you try again?"

Suzanna stood up. "If you'll wait a few minutes, I need to talk to a few people."

"I'm in no hurry," KC assured her.

"Good. I shouldn't be long." When Suzanna left, KC slumped into her chair. Her head hurt, and she felt drained.

Fifteen minutes later, Suzanna returned. Her face gave nothing away.

"Good news or bad?" KC asked, unable to stand the suspense.

Suzanna smiled as she sorted through papers, making them here and there. "Good news. I've convinced my boss to go out on a limb for your mom. The bank will make one more loan, but they're building in a large balloon payment to protect their investment. It's a rather sizable payment, but it's not due right away. It'll give your mother the ski season to bring in some income."

"What happens if she doesn't make the entire amount of the payment?" KC asked warily.

"She'll make it." Suzanna looked at KC, her eyes warm and friendly. "Every hotel in this area is busy between Christmas and New Year's. Your mother will just need to sign these papers." She handed KC the papers she'd been marking.

"Thank you so much," KC said happily as she got up.

"It's my pleasure. And remember what I've told you about Jeremy."

"I'll keep it in mind," KC assured her. "And thank you for being so honest with me."

"You're welcome. Believe me, you'll be glad you steered clear of him."

Twelve

"Nooooh, cool leggings!" Liza cooed, picking up a pair of paisley leggings from Kimberly's open dresser drawer. "Why don't you wear these on your big ski date?"

"They're not warm enough, and it's not a big ski date," Kimberly said flatly as she pulled Faith's nubby green wool sweater over her head.

"It's a professionally guided ski adventure," added Faith, who was rummaging through her own dresser drawer. "Found it," she said, pulling out a wide white headband and tossing it to Kimberly.

Liza took Kimberly's leggings and held them up in front of her. "These might look good on me," she speculated. "Could I borrow them for Winter Carnival this Saturday?"

Kimberly and Faith threw back their heads and howled like coyotes. "Stop that!" Liza demanded, stamping her foot. They'd been doing that to her ever since the night in The Hungry Horse when Coyote had asked her to be his partner at the snowman contest.

"Cut it out!" Liza cried, breaking into a smile. The two girls just howled even louder.

After another moment, their howling dissolved into a fit of laughter. "Sorry, Liza," Faith panted, "but it's hard not to tease you. You sure have changed your opinion of Coyote. It seems to me you just can't wait for this snowman contest."

"I can wait," said Liza. "And it's a woman's perogative to change her mind. Everyone knows that."

"What made you change it?" Kimberly asked.

"I simply saw a different side to him the other night," Liza told them. "It doesn't mean he's the love of my life. But he's okay to build a snowman with."

"Oh, I think you're not telling us the whole truth," Faith needled in a singsong voice. "You've gone head-over-heels for him, haven't you?"

"Not the way Kimberly has fallen for Casper," Liza countered.

"No way." Kimberly laughed. "Casper's not the geek I first thought he was, but he's still too preppy for me. I like a more athletic type, somebody more . . . I don't know . . . more . . ."

"More macho?" Faith asked.

"No, not macho," Kimberly considered. "More guyish, I guess."

"What's the difference?" asked Faith.

"One's obnoxious and the other is cool," Kimberly replied.

Just then, Winnie popped her head into the door. "Did I hear someone talk about my hero, Casper?" she asked, bouncing onto Kimberly's bed.

"We were discussing his guyishness rating," Faith told her. "You know, whether he's macho enough, in a cool way, of course."

"Any guy who's willing to wait tables is guyish enough for me," Winnie said emphatically. "And if the turkey is overcooked or there's a mistake, you can all blame him instead of me."

"Why should we blame him?" asked Kimberly.

"Because he *is* a guy and guys are always the ones who screw up," Winnie explained as if it were a perfectly rational explanation. "That's why he's my hero."

"I thought the term for that was scapegoat," said Faith.

"One person's scapegoat is another person's hero," Winnie said with a philosophical air.

"Winnie, can I borrow your heavy gloves?" Kimberly asked.

"Sure." Winnie tumbled off the bed. "Come to my room and I'll get them for you."

"Thanks. I didn't exactly come prepared to be a professional ski guide."

"Wait for me," Faith called, hurrying after them as they left the room.

Liza sat at the foot of Faith's bed. "'Bye," she said, wiggling her fingers sadly at the open door. They had all just run out and left her sitting there. She looked around her. The room was so different from the whirlwind of tossed clothing in the room she shared with Winnie. To be honest, she had to admit most of the mess was hers. She'd simply never gotten the knack for neatness. It wasn't in her.

But these two sure had it. Everything was so orderly. Liza's eyes fell onto Faith's address book, the only item sitting on the night table between the two single beds. Naturally, Faith had all her numbers neatly collected in one book, unlike Liza, who had hers on scraps of paper stuck here and there.

Picking up the book, Liza flipped through the pages, envious that Faith had so many friends. Her eyes caught a familiar name—a movie star's name. Alec Brady.

That was when Coyote's suggestion came back to her. A movie-star guest *would* be just the thing to draw business to the ranch. It was surefire. But Faith was too proud to call Alec—even if the survival of the ranch depended on it. After they'd gone to see *The Last Ride*, Faith had simply shrugged and said she thought the plot was weak, but that Alec had been pretty good. *If it had been me*, Liza thought, *I would have been up there kissing the screen like a maniac.*

"But I'm not too proud," she said aloud. "If I call Alec, business here will boom. Everyone will say I saved the ranch."

But where could she call from? Not the front desk; it was always busy.

Suddenly, Liza snapped her fingers. Casper's room! She'd seen him carry a fax machine up the stairs when he came. It might have a phone on it.

Feeling like the heroine in a spy movie, Liza slipped out of the room and stole toward Casper's door. She knocked, and when no one answered, she opened the unlocked door. No Casper. He must have already gone off with Kimberly.

She stepped inside and closed the door. The fax

machine sat on his organized desk next to his laptop and a pocket microphone.

There was a phone on the fax.

She picked up the handset and punched in Alec Brady's number. *You have reached Alec Brady,* the phone machine said after four rings. *Unless you've called to annoy me, please leave a message at the tone.*

Suddenly, Liza heard the sound of Winnie calling her, coupled with the slamming of doors. If she was caught, how would she explain this?

The tone beeped piercingly in her ear.

She had to talk. She couldn't just breathe nervously into Alec Brady's phone machine.

"This is Faith's friend . . . um . . . Winnie Gottlieb," she spoke in a frantic rush. "Faith asked me to call you and invite you to her friend's ranch in Montana for Christmas. It's the Angel Dude Ranch in the town of Towerton."

"Liza!" Winnie's voice was getting closer.

"Call four oh six, five, five, five, three, one, two, four. 'Bye."

Winnie rapped sharply on Casper's door. "Anyone in there? Liza?" she called.

Liza ducked down below Casper's bed, praying Winnie wouldn't open the door. Barely daring to breathe, she waited until she heard Winnie's footsteps move down the stairs again. Then she let her breath out in a whoosh.

You chicken, she berated herself for leaving Winnie's name. Oh, well, it didn't matter. The outcome would be the same. And when Alec came bringing fans, the press, and more guests than the ranch could handle, Liza would admit she was the one who had called him.

"I'm sorry about this, I truly am," Winnie told the hen in front of her. "But I've been sent here to collect eggs, so that's what I have to do."

The hen clucked fretfully as Winnie picked up two eggs from the straw. All her life Winnie had eaten eggs without a moment's thought. Now she was filled with remorse at having to rob these hens of their potential offspring. It seemed so unfair. Yet the whole world ate eggs. No one thought it was a particularly heinous crime.

That's why Josh was so good for her. He didn't sweat the small stuff. She missed him terribly. Being separated made her feel like part of her own self was missing. She hadn't expected to feel this way, but she did—oddly out-to-sea and incomplete without him.

"You'll see Josh soon," she consoled herself, scooping up another egg. And the ranch would get customers now that it was snowing. And everything would be fine.

It was important to keep a positive outlook.

And everyone will stop blaming me for everything because I'm not going to make any more mistakes, she resolved.

Her spirits lifting, Winnie put the last egg in her basket. "Thanks, hens," she said as she left the coop. Outside, the cold was biting after the warm damp air of the coop. A light snow still fell all around.

As Winnie made her way back to the lodge she saw Mrs. Angeletti also approaching the side door. KC's mother walked with a spring in her step that Winnie hadn't seen since they'd arrived. "Hi," Winnie called to her.

Mrs. Angeletti smiled and waved back.

"You look happy," Winnie observed when Mrs. Angeletti was near. She was glad to see her smiling.

"Cautiously optimistic, as the politicians say," Mrs. Angeletti told her, smiling. "I just came in from downtown, where I was signing the papers for my revised, extended, expanded loan. It really gives me some breathing space. I don't know how KC did it."

"All those business courses are paying off," Winnie said. Saying this made Winnie feel very mature and magnanimous. Up until now she'd never thought much of KC's decision to major in business. To Winnie, there was much more to life than making money. But right now there was no denying that KC's business acumen was paying off, and Winnie wasn't too small to admit it.

"I guess so," said Mrs. Angeletti. As she spoke she thumbed through a stack of mail in her gloved hand. "Now, here's the *bad* news," she added, frowning. "I just grabbed the mail on my way in, and I have a new stack of bills. Half of them are overdue notices and—"

Suddenly Mrs. Angeletti went pale.

"A really whomping bill?" Winnie asked.

Mrs. Angeletti didn't seem to hear her. With trembling hands she tore open a long envelope and read what appeared to be a letter.

"What is it?" Winnie asked, worried by the tense, angry expression that was taking form on Mrs. Angeletti's face.

"This is from Lewiston Tower," Mrs. Angeletti said. "He says you girls crashed his party. Is this true?"

"Well, yeah," Winnie admitted sheepishly.

"Apparently he's furious about it and says he considers it a personal insult. He says he intends to pay the insult back in kind."

"What does that mean?"

"I have no idea, Winnie." Mrs. Angeletti spoke with an edge of panic in her voice. "It could mean anything! Anything! All I know for sure is that it's not good. How could you girls have done such a thing?"

"We didn't think it was a big deal. Besides, he deserved an insult after the things he's done to you," Winnie replied defensively.

"That may be so. However, I'm in no position to lock horns with Lewiston Tower."

"But aren't you mad about the horse incident?" Winnie pressed.

"Why can't you girls just forget about that?" Mrs. Angeletti said, her voice rising. "Whose idea was it to crash the party, anyway? Was it that Liza's?"

"No," Winnie said quickly.

"Then whose?"

Winnie stood silently. *For your information, it was KC's big idea!* she thought. But she would never rat on her friend.

Tears rushed to Mrs. Angeletti's eyes. "As I remember, Winnie, back in high school these sorts of pranks were usually instigated by you."

"Me!?" Winnie yelped indignantly. "Why is everything my fault?" Blinded by her own tears, Winnie rushed away, not sure where she was running to.

But one thing she did know. She had to get away from this place where no one trusted or appreciated her. She wasn't sure how she would do it, but she had to flee. In all her life, she'd never felt as wrongfully picked on and abused as she did on this trip.

Thirteen

"Come on, you can do it," Kimberly coaxed Casper's Rent-a-Wreck Chevette up the icy road. The car coughed in reply, but kept climbing. She and Casper were returning from town, where they'd just rented their boots and poles.

"Could that ski-shop guy have been any happier to see us?" Casper laughed from behind the steering wheel. "You'd think we were his long-lost children or something."

Kimberly smiled, remembering how the man had fawned over them, welcoming them to his shop. "I guess a lot of businesses around here suffer when there's a bad ski season," she said.

"Isn't that the Tower Ranch to our right?" said Casper, pointing.

Peering out the frosty window, Kimberly saw the rooftop of the Tower barn down in what seemed to be a valley. The road did indeed border Tower property. She gazed up ahead at the entrance to the Rocky Peak ski area. "I wonder if they own Rocky Peak," she said apprehensively.

"Don't worry. I doubt they're standing at the entrance inspecting each car that comes through."

"I wouldn't put it past them," Kimberly grumbled.

Casper laughed. "Besides, they've never seen me and they probably don't remember you from the dance."

"Oh, they'll remember this face," Kimberly said with grim confidence.

"Well, I wouldn't easily forget such a beautiful face. That's true," said Casper, his eyes still on the road.

Kimberly turned to look at him. "Thanks," she said. "But I meant they wouldn't forget a black face. I haven't seen another black person since we got here."

"I guess if I were the only white person for miles, I might feel self-conscious, too," he admitted. "But, then again, maybe I wouldn't. It would depend on how people treated me."

"That's the thing of it," Kimberly said. "When you go into unfamiliar territory and you're a minority, you're never really sure what kind of reaction you're going to get." It was so easy to talk to him, and this wasn't a subject Kimberly always felt comfortable discussing.

"It's a shame people are so stupid about stuff like that." Casper sighed. "They really limit themselves."

"What's so annoying is that people make assumptions about who you are, and they have no idea what they're talking about," Kimberly said.

They pulled past a sign that read "Rocky Peak," and continued into a parking area. "Ski season isn't booming yet," Kimberly remarked, noting that the lot was only half full.

Casper stopped the car and checked his watch. "Maybe the early birds have come and gone. It's almost three."

With their gear in tow, they headed over toward the ski area. "I didn't get in much skiing last year," Kimberly admitted as she looked up at Rocky Peak, which seemed to disappear into the clouds. "I should probably test my legs a little before we go up the lift."

"No problem. I don't care if we stay on the foothills. Remember, I'm a complete beginner."

"I thought you prep-school types always went

away on fabulous ski holidays to Switzerland, and all."

"Now who's making assumptions?" Casper challenged.

"Sorry," Kimberly apologized. She looked around at the skiers who dotted the mountainside. "Mrs. Angeletti was right," she commented. "This is a pretty no-frills spot. There's no lodge, no rental place. Just a mountain and a lift."

"That's all you need, isn't it?" said Casper as he worked at stepping into his skies.

"Yeah, but a cup of hot cocoa after skiing would be nice," Kimberly countered.

"The galloping gourmet is on the case. I've got it covered," he said with a smile. "There's a full thermos in the car, and some snacks."

"All right!" Kimberly cheered softly. "Good thinking."

They began skiing on the foothills surrounding Rocky Peak. Kimberly was relieved to discover that her body hadn't forgotten the feeling of skiing. It all came back to her.

Casper was another story. He flailed his arms wildly. His ski tips seemed magnetized and were continually meeting, then crosssing, sending him crashing into the snow.

"Don't get discouraged," Kimberly said, laughing. She extended her hand to pull him up.

"You're still locking your legs. Remember to keep your knees bent and loose."

"There's too much to think about in this sport," he mumbled as he wiped his wet glasses. "You make it look so easy."

"I did my share of falling when I was first learning," she said kindly. But the truth was, Kimberly could never remember having as difficult a time as Casper. He seemed to have no natural athletic ability at all.

Within half an hour, he managed to collide with her three times. The third time he caught her off guard and sent her toppling into the snow. "Are you doing this on purpose?" She laughed, picking up a handful of snow and tossing it at him.

He responded by tossing snow back at her. "Maybe I am," he said, throwing more snow her way. "Some mysterious force keeps drawing me to you."

"Yeah, well, crash-into-Kimberly is not one of the ways to stop your downhill run."

"Oh, I thought it was," he teased. "So sorry."

They got up and brushed the snow from themselves.

"You're just so pretty," Casper said without embarrassment. "Watching you move reminds me of a deer."

Kimberly wasn't sure what to say. Usually her

quick tongue served her well, but right now she didn't want to spoil things with a joke. She just looked at him and smiled quietly. He smiled back, and a wordless connection seemed to run between them.

By four thirty the sun was low in the sky, and a shiver ran up Kimberly's spine. She watched Casper go slowly down the hill behind her. He had made a lot of progress in the last hour. At least he was managing to stay up.

"How was that?" he asked when he reached the bottom of the hill.

Kimberly smiled. "You're a fast learner."

"This must be getting boring for you," he said. "Want to try the lift?"

"Okay, we'll just go to the midstation. The slopes shouldn't be too difficult from there."

"I'm ready," he said gamely.

"We'll probably have time for only one run," she said as they pushed themselves along toward the lift. "Unless they have night skiing."

"No." Casper shook his head. "I saw a sign that said the lifts stop at five thirty."

"The place is clearing out already," Kimberly said, noticing that only a few skiers were making their way down from the mountain trails. When they got to the lift, there was no line. They paid the attendant and got onto the next chair.

"Isn't this amazing," she said as the chair swayed gently on its way up the mountainside. Below her the slopes were tinged with pink from the setting sun. The majestic pines rustled softly.

"How can just a cable hold this chair up?" Casper fretted, looking at the thick cable that carried them along. "I can never understand that. Suspension bridges make me antsy, too. I just don't get the cable concept. I mean, they look so flimsy."

Kimberly shrugged. She'd never thought much about it. "I'm sure it's safe."

"Rationally, I believe you," Casper said shakily. "But I just keep trying to estimate how far down we would fall if this thing collapsed."

"Not far. About sixteen feet, maybe twenty," she estimated. "But this thing isn't going to collapse. It's perfectly safe."

Suddenly Kimberly was lurched forward in her seat. Instinctively she clutched the safety bar. Then her neck snapped back as the chair jerked to a halt.

"You were saying?" said Casper dryly. His pale, anxious face belied his ironic tone. His eyes darted between her face and the cable that held the chair.

"I'm sure we'll get started in a minute." Kimberly rubbed the back of her neck. "Somebody below us probably dropped a ski, or had trouble getting on."

Casper checked his watch. "It's only four thirty. They wouldn't have shut the lift already, would they?"

"Of course not. They saw us get on."

"Right. They know we're here."

"That's right," Kimberly agreed. She swiveled around to see what was going on behind her, but they had come over a mountain ledge which dipped down sharply, obscuring any view of the bottom. Below, a couple skied past.

"Hey," Casper called to them. "We're stuck!"

Kimberly sunk down in the seat, embarrassed. "I'm sure they know the lift isn't moving, Casper."

"I'm sorry, but I don't like dangling in the middle of thin air."

"Just keep a positive attitude."

"Oh, excuse me, Wonder Woman, but I'd rather not freeze to death up here!"

"You're not going to freeze to death!" Kimberly snapped. She was getting nervous, and he wasn't helping the situation.

"You've been implying that I'm a wimp since I got here," he snapped back. "I don't know what kind of caveman image you have of me, but I'm happy with myself just the way I am. Okay?"

Kimberly was stunned by his outburst. Reluctantly, she admitted to herself that it was probably warranted. Being stuck up here was not only making him anxious, it was making her panicky and snappish, too. "Okay," she said.

They sat dangling their skis helplessly as the wind picked up, rocking the chair back and forth. In the dying light, another skier went past them. "Hey! Help!" Casper shouted. "Up here."

This time Kimberly joined him. "We're stuck! Get help!" she called to the skier. The man waved up to them as he whizzed past. Kimberly hoped he'd heard them, but she wasn't sure.

An unexpected chill caused Kimberly to shiver. Casper put his arm around her and rubbed her arm. She smiled at him, glad he wasn't still angry. Things were bad enough without them fighting. The glorious sunset was fading into darkness.

"I say we get out of here," Casper said.

"How could we possibly?"

Casper pulled off his parka. "If we tied the sleeves of our jackets together and climbed down, I bet the drop to the bottom wouldn't be too bad."

"Think so?" Kimberly peered dubiously over the side.

"I don't know. Someone will be along soon."

"I'll wait fifteen more minutes, then I say we go," he replied.

The longest fifteen minutes Kimberly had ever

known slowly passed. No new skiers whooshed by, and a gray glow over the trees was all that remained of the sun. Now the wind whipped fiercely around them. Kimberly shivered more from fright than from the cold.

"That's it," Casper announced firmly. "I'm going down first and you're coming right after me. Take off your jacket."

Wordlessly, Kimberly unzipped her jacket and handed it to him. The wind cut through her sweater, but she tried not to think about it.

His teeth chattering, Casper knotted the sleeves of their jackets together and then tied one sleeve to the bottom rung of the chair. "Will it hold our weight?" she asked.

"I was a Boy Scout," Casper said with a quick smile. "I was good at two things: camp fire cooking and knots. The knots will hold; it's the fabric that might not."

"The fabric might not," Kimberly echoed. This was insanity. They were just asking for cracked skulls.

"But it probably will hold," he said, patting her arm briskly. "As soon as I get to the bottom, you come down." He unlocked the safety bar and slid down on his jacket.

"Careful," Kimberly murmured as she watched him disappear below her. Straining to see, she leaned forward and watched his descent. His skis banged together and the chair rocked as he went. *He should have undone his skis before he went,* she thought. *What if they lock and he breaks his leg when he drops?* She wouldn't be able to get him off the mountain. He'd freeze. They both would. How had a simple ski trip turned into such a nightmare? Why hadn't anyone come to check on them?

After a few more breathless moments, he reached the bottom of her jacket. "Geronimo!" he yelled as he let go and fell to the ground. Kimberly sucked in her breath, waiting to see if he'd get up.

Finally, he did, clutching his right shoulder. "Your turn!" he called up to her.

Kimberly undid her ski bindings and let her skis dangle from her boots by their safety straps. She pushed herself to the edge of the chair and sat looking down at the jackets dancing in the wind. She'd never been great at rope climbing in gym. Could she make it?

"Come on!" Casper shouted up at her. "The first step is the hardest."

He wasn't kidding. She wasn't sure it was a step she could take. It looked like such a long way down.

"Don't wimp out on me now, Wonder Woman!" Casper called up to her.

Kimberly wasn't sure if it was the taunt of being called a wimp, or the image of herself as Wonder Woman, but his words got her moving. She pulled off her gloves and tucked them into her jeans pocket. Clutching the jacket sleeve, she lowered herself down onto the slippery fabric. Every muscle in her body was taut as she concentrated on keeping hold of the cloth.

She was halfway down when a sickening sound filled her head. The cloth was ripping. She looked up and saw that the fabric near the top knot had torn. Now, with every second, the tear was widening.

"Keep coming!" Casper coached. "Don't stop!"

His soothing tone got her going again. "You're almost there," he continued. "I'm right here. You're not far from the ground now." She let his voice carry her. He seemed to sense this and kept up the steady patter of comforting words.

In moments, her feet kicked out into the air. She was coming to the end of the rope. Again, an icy panic ran through her. She couldn't let go. "I'll catch you," he called.

Riiip!

The torn fabric made the decision for her. It gave way, sending Kimberly hurtling to the ground.

"I've got you!" cried Casper.

With a thud, she fell on top of him. He buckled under the impact, sending them both careening to the ground.

The fall had knocked Casper's glasses off, and Kimberly found herself staring right into his eyes. "You okay?" he asked.

Kimberly ran a quick check. "I'm fine," she said, and—filled with relief and gratitude—she kissed him.

He wrapped his left hand around her shoulder and kissed back. Kimberly felt wonderful. When she pulled back, they smiled at each other. Then Casper's expression twisted into a cringe. "What's wrong?" she asked, rolling off him.

"My shoulder, or maybe it's my collarbone. I can't tell," he said. "I hit it when I fell. I think something is cracked or fractured or who knows what."

"Oh, no." Kimberly quickly got to her feet. "Let's get out of here."

He got up beside her and picked up their jackets off the ground. Unknotting the sleeves, he handed her hers. "At least we won't get lost," he said. "We can follow the chair-lift path back down."

Just then, a single beam of light cut through the darkness and the sound of a snowmobile engine filled the air. "Finally!" Kimberly cried, quickly rebuckling her skis.

Up over a ridge, the snowmobile came into sight. Kimberly and Casper skied toward it. As the driver neared them, Kimberly stiffened. She recognized the driver's squinting eyes and blond ponytail.

It was Jake Tower.

He pulled to a stop beside them. From his stony expression, Kimberly knew he wasn't there to check on their health.

"What happened?" Kimberly asked with guarded anger. "The lift shut down early."

"I turned it off," he replied.

Kimberly gasped. "You what? Who do you think you are?"

"This is Tower land. We control everything that happens here."

"Didn't you know we were on the lift?" Casper shouted angrily.

Jake eyed Casper dispassionately. "Yep. I knew."

"And you left us hanging there?" Casper shouted in disbelief.

Jake sat back in his seat and folded his arms. "Listen, you two, and listen good. I control the lift. It's the only one around here. It goes off when I say it does, and on when I say it does. You tell your boss lady that it's staying off."

"That's insane!" Kimberly shouted. "No one will come here to ski. You'll ruin your own business. You'll hurt everyone in the entire area, not just Mrs. Angeletti!"

"We'll survive," Jake replied. "We're not hurting for money."

"You're a monster!" Kimberly shrieked at him. "A spiteful, hateful monster!"

Jake shook his head slowly. "Call me what you like, but this was just a warning. Your family has upset my grandfather, and what upsets him upsets me. From here on, the Towers are through playing games." With a flurry of snow, he hit the motor and zoomed away from them.

"Man," said Casper. "You're right, that guy is insane. He's willing to destroy the ski season in the whole area just to drive Mrs. Angeletti out of business. Not to mention what he just did to us. I wonder if he ever would have let us down."

A sickening knot was forming in Kimberly's stomach. "I wonder, too," she said.

How far were the Towers willing to go to destroy the Angel Ranch?

Fourteen

K C sipped her hot cocoa as she, Faith, Liza, and Winnie listened to Kimberly and Casper's astonishing tale of their encounter with Jake Tower. With every word Kimberly spoke, she could feel herself becoming more and more outraged. "That family is out of control," she said when Kimberly was done. "You guys could have been seriously hurt. Where is this going to end?"

"Do you really think he would destroy the whole ski season just to get at your mom?" Faith asked, stoking the fire in the stone fireplace. "That's so outrageous that it's unbelievable. If it's true, it's scary."

"No kidding, it is scary," Casper agreed. "The Towers are a family of psychos, if you ask me." He sat beside Kimberly with his shoulder taped and his arm cradled in a sling. He and Kimberly had driven all the way to the hospital in Grand Falls, where a doctor had fixed Casper's dislocated shoulder.

"I wish I'd had my pocket tape recorder with me," Casper went on. "If I could have recorded what Jake Tower said to us, we could take it to the papers, let this whole town know how much the Towers really care about them."

"What do you have that pocket recorder for, anyway?" Liza questioned from where she sat draped across two chairs.

"I carry it with me to record ideas for the paper I'm working on," he explained. "It's like carrying a notepad, only handier."

"What else would you expect from Mr. Electronics?" Kimberly teased. "This guy even needs a fax machine just to write a school paper."

Casper smiled. "I know it looks excessive, but I borrowed it from my sister's office. It helps me get information I need from the Yale library."

"Wow! You mean they'll really send you stuff," cried Winnie, who was sitting at a table writing a letter as she listened.

KC couldn't believe how easily they'd shifted to

another subject. Her mother's whole life was crashing in, and they were chitchatting about the wonder of modern electronics. Obviously they didn't see the seriousness of the situation. How could they? KC conceded. She hadn't actually told them how dire her mother's financial situation was. They didn't realize that the entire ranch could go under if it didn't begin to fill up with guests soon. If the Towers kept the only lift in town closed, it meant utter ruin for her mother. All the snow in the world didn't matter if people couldn't ski.

"Listen, everybody, this lift business is very serious," she broke into their conversation. "Nobody tell my mom about it, okay? When she comes back from Christmas shopping, just act like everything is fine."

"Shouldn't she know?" Liza questioned.

"Not now, with the big dinner tomorrow night," KC replied. "The snow has really lifted her spirits, and I think she'd go into the dinner with a better attitude if she didn't know this depressing news."

"Desperation tends to show," Liza agreed. "And it's pretty unattractive. It makes people nervous. You're right, ignorance can be bliss."

"One of the merchants might tell her, though," said Winnie quietly.

KC pondered this. Winnie had a point. And it might not be good if her mother found out in the middle of the dinner. Still, KC's instincts told her to let it be for the moment. Her mother was under enough pressure.

There was another possibility slowly taking form in her mind. Maybe she could fix the problem before her mother ever found out about it. There was one person she knew would listen to her. Jeremy. Even if he was a loser and a bully, as Suzanna said, he would let her talk. He might even try to help her, if she could get through to him. She had to try.

"I still say we shouldn't tell her," KC said.

Winnie shrugged. "Suit yourself. If she does find out about it, she didn't hear it from me. Wild horses couldn't drag it out of me. I'll be quiet as a tomb. Mute. Silent as the grave. Speechless. Completely unforthcoming with information. Absolutely—"

"All right, Winnie!" Faith cut her off. "We got the message."

"Good," Winnie huffed. "Because I'm tired of being blamed for things."

"Are you still mad about the soup thing?" KC asked her. "I thought it had all blown over, but maybe I was—"

"Forget it," Winnie grumbled. "It's not important."

"We'd better start prepping for the dinner tomorrow, like we planned," Faith said.

"We'll help." Kimberly gestured to herself and Casper.

"All right," KC said, getting up from her chair. She was about to follow Kimberly and Casper into the kitchen when she suddenly snapped her fingers. She'd almost forgotten about the Winter Carnival the next day. "Oh no! No one will be available to work on the cleanup committee at the carnival tomorrow. We'll all have to be here working on the dinner," she cried. "Liza, would you go? Somebody *has* to. It's a business-community committee, and we can't let them down. You'll be at the carnival anyway."

Liza slumped in her chair. "Oh, please, please, please don't make me do that," she begged. "It'll be so humiliating! I can just hear myself: 'Oh, 'bye, Coyote, I have to go now and clean up everyone else's slop.' How embarrassing. Besides, I didn't volunteer for this stupid thing. You did."

"I know *I* signed up, but I wasn't thinking about all the preparation that would be needed here," KC explained, working hard to control her temper. "Liza, you have to! Please! All you have to do is sign in and—" Just then, the sound of the phone ringing in the lobby cut KC off.

"I'll get it," said Faith.

KC crossed her fingers. "Oh, please let it be a reservation," she prayed.

"Hello, Angel Dude Ranch," Faith answered the phone.

"Hi, is Faith there, please," a male voice requested.

"Who's calling?" Faith asked, wondering who this was.

"Is that you, Faith? It's me, Alec."

"Alec?" Faith asked, her mind a blank. "Alec Brady?"

"Yeah. Hi! How have you been? Sorry I haven't been in touch, but my life has been completely wild. We wrapped one movie and then I went right into another. I don't know which way is up these days. So, how's it going?"

"Fine. I mean . . . fine." Faith breathed deeply, trying to calm down. If this was a joke, whoever was playing it did a perfect Alec Brady imitation. Absolutely perfect.

Faith's heart began to pound. She'd convinced herself she didn't care if she if she ever saw Alec again—convinced herself that she *would* never see him again. Their relationship had been thrilling, but he was a huge movie star. She wasn't going to go around all stars truck and mopey about him. Yet now that she heard his voice again, all the old excitement came rushing back.

But how had he gotten her number? *She* hadn't even known it until they got here. None of this made sense.

"It was great to hear from you after so long. When I got your message I felt like a real jerk for not being in touch," he went on. "Do you forgive me?"

"Sure, of course," Faith replied, confused. "But what message are you talking about?"

"The one your friend Winnie Gottlieb left for me. How come she called instead of you? Is everything okay?"

Winnie!? She'd never given Winnie Alec's number. Faith's mind went into high gear trying to make sense of this. "Winnie called you?"

"Yeah. Didn't you know?"

"No . . . I . . . I . . . Well, it's good to talk to you, anyway," she said. "What did Winnie actually say?"

"She said you wanted me to come up and visit. But I don't think I can. I've got to be in Paris until the end of the month. I'm in an action-thriller thing. It's awesome, really. I get to run all over the Eiffel Tower chasing this half-robot, half-alien double-agent spy. The plot makes no sense.

Which is why it'll probably be a big hit. But there's a slim, slim, slim chance the shoot will be delayed until January, so tell me exactly where you are."

"All right." Faith gave him the directions as if she were in a trance. She was so stunned by the call that it all seemed a little unreal. Even the sound of her own voice sounded unfamiliar.

On the other end of the phone, Faith heard someone call to Alec. "Okay! Okay! I'll be right there," he shouted back. "Makeup people," he griped to Faith. "They think they're the most important people on the entire set. Who knows? Maybe they are. Anyway, I gotta fly. If there's any way I can make it out there, I'll let you know. Take care of yourself, Faith."

"You too. 'Bye," Faith said dreamily. She leaned against the desk, trying to understand what had just happened. Winnie had left a message saying that she, Faith, wanted him to visit her? How could she do such a thing?

Faith had taken such pride in keeping her dignity and not chasing him—not degrading herself by acting like a fame-mad groupie. At times it had taken steely self-control to keep from contacting him. It had been really hard, but she'd managed. And now—with one phone call—Winnie had undone all that. Winnie had cast Faith in the very light she dreaded being seen in.

Was she secretly glad, though? Faith asked herself. No. Alec had no intention of coming here. He probably wasn't even going to Paris at all. He was just trying to let her down easy. How humiliating! How mortifying!

"Winnie!" Faith bellowed, storming into the dining room.

Dear Josh, Winnie wrote. *This trip was really a bad idea. I can't wait to see you again. So far KC exploded at me in front of everyone because I made one small mistake in a recipe. Mrs. Angeletti has accused me of being the mastermind behind everything that has ever gone wrong in the world. We're being victimized by a demonic, berserk family, and everyone is extremely, mondo tense. Right now I am sitting here in the dining room being ogled by the glassy-eyed heads of murdered, decapitated wildlife and a ferocious-looking stuffed grizzly, listening to KC bickering with Liza about who is going to go to the cleanup committee that KC signed up for. I love KC, but she's really getting on my nerves this trip. Oh, here's a happy new development. Faith just came flying in looking bug-eyed, like her head is about to explode any second. I wonder what's—*

Winnie put her pen down as she realized Faith was barreling toward her like a bull about to charge. All Winnie could think of was those cartoons where characters got so mad they actually had steam blasting out of their ears. "What's wrong?" she asked.

"How could you call Alec Brady?" Faith demanded. "You have some nerve."

"What are you talking about?" Winnie asked.

"That was Alec Brady on the phone. He got the message *you* left for him saying that *I* wanted to see him."

Winnie had never seen Faith this enraged. "Excuse me, but I don't have the slightest idea of what you are talking about. I never called Alec Brady."

"Don't lie, Winnie! Alec told me you called him!"

"Winnie! You didn't!" KC gasped, breaking off her conversation with Liza.

Tears of indignant anger rose in Winnie's eyes. "No. I didn't." This was the last straw. She was sick and tired of being continually blamed for things she hadn't done. "Did it ever occur to you that Alec Brady is the one who might be lying?" she shouted.

"Why would he do that?" Faith scoffed.

"Maybe he felt he needed an excuse to call you after so much time. Maybe he's a psychopathic liar. How do I know?" Winnie realized she was shouting and crying, but she didn't care. Let them see how much they'd hurt her. What kind of friends were these who would assume the worst about her? This was a total betrayal.

"Alec isn't like that," Faith insisted.

"Oh, but I am! Is that it?" Winnie yelled, tearfully picking up her letter to Josh. "It's good to finally know what you really think of me."

"Maybe he just got mixed up," Liza offered, looking extremely uncomfortable. "You know how wacky those Hollywood types are. Let's get back to this cleanup committee thing. I just really can't do it."

Winnie was amazed. Here were her two so-called best friends attacking her, and she got more sympathy from Liza, whom she wasn't even that close to. "Don't worry about it, Liza," Winnie said. "I'll do it. Since everyone around here dumps on me, it's fitting that the whole town should do it, too. And then, after that, I'm taking the next bus out of here. You won't have to worry about Winnie Gottlieb flakiness wrecking your precious plans."

Fighting back tears, Winnie whirled around and stormed out of the dining room. With any luck, she could catch a plane and be with Josh for Christmas.

With luck, she'd never have to speak to KC or Faith—or any of them—again as long as she lived.

Fifteen

·······/··········

Early the next morning, Liza stood on the front porch and watched Winnie drag her big canvas bag through the falling snow over to Casper's car. Winnie hadn't spoken to anyone since the night before. She'd even taken her things from the room she and Liza shared and gone to sleep in an empty guest room.

Liza knew she owed it to Winnie to tell the truth. But the coward in her was winning right now. The words wouldn't come. And, after all, maybe it didn't matter if she spoke up. That wasn't really the issue. The issue was the way her friends dumped on Winnie and didn't believe her. Perhaps this was all for the best. Maybe Winnie really needed to make a break with them. If that was so, nothing would be gained by Liza speaking up.

Deep in her heart Liza knew she was only giving herself empty rationalizations for what she'd done. The truth was, she'd schemed and lied and now someone else was taking the heat for it. That wasn't fair, especially not to Winnie. Of all of them, Winnie was the nicest. With Winnie, Liza didn't feel as though she was being judged all the time. And now Winnie was going.

Don't be such a self-centered little twit, Liza chided herself. *Coyote may be picking you up in five minutes, but you're not even sure if you like him.* Winnie was certainly more important. Determined to set things straight, Liza walked off the porch. "Hi," she said to Winnie.

Winnie turned and frowned.

"Don't go. Nobody wants you to leave."

"Faith does," Winnie replied. "And so does KC. Her precious dinner is more important than my feelings. KC thinks I'm a flake, Faith thinks I'm a liar, and Kimberly thinks I can't be trusted with a secret. If anything does go wrong, Mrs. Angeletti will blame me. Why stay?"

"Maybe you're just being too sensitive."

Winnie slammed the trunk shut. "Oh, and you think I'm too sensitive."

"No, I don't. Really! I think you're great," Liza said urgently. Why was Winnie making this so difficult? Liza just wanted it over with so she could go back to worrying about her date with Coyote. If Winnie would stay, then the whole thing would blow over and maybe Liza wouldn't have to admit to anything.

"Well, thanks," said Winnie. "Come to think of it, you're the only one who hasn't blamed me or insulted me. You and I should spend more time together when we get back to school."

"I'd like that," Liza said honestly. If Winnie only knew! How could she tell her the truth now— after what she'd just said?

Winnie began wiping snow from the windshield. It had begun snowing only two hours earlier and already there was almost two inches of snow on the car. "Are you sure you want to drive this heap?" Liza asked, trying another approach. "What if you get stuck on the road and die of frostbite or something?"

"I'm not going too far. Casper said I could leave the car at the bus station and he'd find it. He's a sweet guy."

"Yeah. But don't you think it would be safer if you waited and rode down to the carnival in Kimberly's van with the rest of them?"

"I don't want to talk to anyone," Winnie insisted,

brushing snow off her gloves. "Besides, I don't want to have to ask for a lift to the bus station. I don't want to ask anything from my so-called friends." She leaned against the car. "I wonder what the story really was with Alec Brady, because I sure didn't call him."

Here was Liza's chance. This was her opening to tell the truth. The words formed in her head, but somehow they got all bunched up and caught in her throat. This wasn't a very good time to tell the truth, anyway. What if Coyote arrived in the middle of a whole bunch of yelling and screaming? What if he found out what she'd done? "Who knows," was all Liza could manage to say.

"My theory is that Alec wanted an excuse to come see Faith, but he's too proud to just ask, so he made up that story," said Winnie. "He knew I was a friend of Faith's, so he just picked my name out of the blue."

"It makes sense to me," Liza said feebly.

"Me, too. But, of course, Faith would rather think that I pulled some wacky stunt than believe her precious Alec Brady might resort to a little subterfuge. It just hurts my feelings more than I can tell you." Winnie forced a small smile. "I won't say 'bye now, because I'll probably see you down at the Carnival. Good luck with the snowman contest."

"Thanks," said Liza. She was about to wish Winnie good luck with the cleanup committe, but that didn't seem like a good idea. "I'll see you down there," she said instead.

"Yeah." Winnie laughed grimly as she climbed into the car. "I'll be the one with the broom. See ya."

Liza watched Winnie drive off in the old car. She had never felt more like a rat in her life.

Just then, the others came out the front door. They stopped talking as they watched Casper's car disappear out the gate. "One of you could have tried to stop her," Liza attacked them. "I tried, but you're supposed to be her good friends."

"I tried last night, but she wouldn't talk to me," said KC. Faith just looked up at the falling snow.

"You guys will patch things up," said Kimberly. "Everyone just needs a little cooling-down period."

"And meanwhile, with Casper in a sling and Winnie gone, we're two waiters short for the dinner tonight," said KC.

Liza looked at her. Was that all KC cared about? Her dinner? There was no doubt in Liza's mind that KC Angeletti would do just fine for herself in life. She was cold and determined, and cared only about accomplishing what she set out to do.

"Are you coming down with us to the carnival?" Kimberly said as she headed for the van.

"No," Liza answered. "Coyote is supposed to pick me up."

"Okay, well, have fun today," said Faith.

"And please remember to be back in time for the dinner," added KC.

"Will do," said Liza, wiggling her fingers at them as they drove off. She looked up and brushed snow from her hair. It would probably be smart to wear a hat, but she hated winter hats. She didn't have the face for them. She didn't have the hips for the leggings she was wearing, either, but she never let that bother her.

Moving back to the porch, she sat down to wait for Coyote. Her watch told her it was nine forty. He was ten minutes late. Maybe he'd forgotten all about their date and was sleeping late on this snowy day.

"Serves you right," she muttered to herself. After what she'd done to Winnie, she didn't deserve to have a fun day out with a cute guy. This was all probably some nasty joke he'd cooked up to put her in her place.

Hopeful, she waited another five minutes. Then she picked up the paper bag she'd loaded with odds and ends for her snowman and opened the front door. As she was about to close it behind her, the sound of an engine made her stop. A large brown pickup truck was banging through the front gate.

Suddenly her dark mood turned sunny. She bounced out onto the porch, letting the door slam behind her. Coyote waved to her from the truck and she ran toward him, taking in his bright eyes and red mustache as if seeing him for the first time. She'd never noticed his slightly upturned, nicely squared-off nose or the dimple in his chin before. He was actually quite good-looking.

"Sorry I'm late," he apologized as she climbed into the cab of the truck. "We had a real late gig last night and I had a hard time getting the bod in gear this morning."

"No problem," said Liza. "I just now walked out the door myself."

He leaned back in his seat and looked at the ranch. Raising his tawny brows, his eyes danced with merriment. "So this is the happening night spot, huh?" he said with a barely suppressed grin. "I'm glad I was able to get this truck in, what with all the cars parked in the lot. Wow! How are you fitting all the guests in?"

Liza smiled, then frowned, then smiled again. "Oh, what's the use?" she said. "I'm not fooling you. Mrs. Angeletti is just getting started, and she's struggling. But she'll make it."

He pushed her shoulder playfully. "Okay, girl! Now we're getting somewhere. I like honesty, and I *like* those boots. Oooh-eee! Sexy!"

Liza looked down at her stiletto-heeled boots and blushed. She pushed him back. "Let's go build a snowman."

"Yes, ma'am," he said, turning the truck around. He turned on the radio loud as they bumped along the snow-covered road. Liza felt an emotion she barely recognized. She realized she was happy. Full-out happy—here in an old truck with a handsome cowboy who thought she was sexy, or at least that her feet were, with the radio blaring country music on a snowy day. If anyone had asked what it would take to make her happy, this was *not* the scene she'd have described. Not by a long shot. But here she was, and she *was* happy.

Downtown, they hit a traffic jam. Towerton was transformed with colorful banners, rides, food concessions, and floats. Music filled the air, coming from speakers mounted on storefronts. Every type of vehicle from pickups to motorcycles to horses tried to make its way into the narrow street, where police detoured them. The main road was flooded with pedestrians. The ever-more-heavily falling snow had deterred no one from this big event. In fact, Liza thought it lent an air of festivity.

Coyote finally managed to park the truck, and they made their way to the village green where the snowman contest was already under way. The bottoms of at least ten other fat white snowmen dotted the landscape. "Let's get to it," said Coyote, pulling on his heavy gloves. "We have to catch up before the others hog up all the snow."

Liza looked up and laughed. "I think there's a never-ending supply today," she said. She packed a fat snowball, then put it down in the snow and began rolling it. The soft, dry snow was perfect, and before too long they had a good base. "Keep going," Liza said. "This is going to be the fat mama of all snowladies."

"Oh, she's a lady, is she?" Coyote smiled.

"Sure. She's the Queen of the Carnival."

"Queen of the Carnival built by the real queen of the carnival and her humble servant," he teased happily.

Liza looked at him and her heart thumped in delight. How could she have ever disliked him? He was charming and gallant. Full of life! Not knowing how else to respond, she packed a snowball and tossed it at him, sending it skidding off his shoulder.

He responded by throwing a snowball back at her. In minutes, they were engaged in a full-scale snowball fight. "You win! You win!" Liza panted.

"We're wasting time. We have to get back to our mission here."

Coyote laughed and brushed snow from his brown corduroy jacket. He looked around him and his face grew serious. "Oh, yeah, you're right. We're lagging behind. Let's go."

Working on the snowman made Liza forget her nervousness and insecurity. She was transported to the time when she was a kid in Brooklyn and she'd turned all her creativity to bringing these snow creatures to life. Being creative was the only way Liza could forget herself. And today, every fiber of her being was concentrated on the task at hand. Rounding an edge, finding the right angle for the arm, carving out individual fingers: everything had to be just right.

Slowly the mammoth lady grew. First the base, then the midsection and then the head, until the tall Coyote could barely pat the snow onto her head. "She needs a face as bright as the sun," Liza said. "She is the queen, after all." She dug in her bag for a spool of red ribbon. "Let's give her a bright-red smile."

They gave her a wide smile and a coal nose. Liza had found some dusty old plastic flowers in a closet at the ranch, so the snowwoman got daisy eyes with jet-black centers, the petals forming lavish lashes. "Do you think she's a redhead?" Liza asked as she inspected the bag of carrots she'd brought along for props.

"Of course she is," Coyote replied, taking off his cowboy hat and running a hand through his own carrot-top. "All the best people are."

He smiled directly at her, engaging her eyes in a way that gave his words added impact. What exactly was he saying? she wondered. That they were two of a kind? That she was one of the best people?

"I couldn't agree more," said Liza softly as she twirled one of her own red curls around her finger.

By virtue of his height, Coyote got the job of jumping up and placing each carrot until the snowwoman had a head full of spiky orange hair. The rest of the ribbon went to making a necklace. Coyote ran around the back of a store and returned with an armful of berry-flecked holly that he'd picked from a bush. The snowwoman was given a spray of it to hold, and the rest went to adorn her carrot-hair. He ran back to his truck and found an old flowered sheet and tied it as a scarf around her neck.

"I have the finishing touch!" Liza cried gleefully. She pulled a card of long, bright-red press-on nails from her bag. "I knew these would come in handy someday," she said as she pressed each nail into the snowwoman's hands. "This isn't exactly what I had in mind for them, but . . ."

"She's beautiful!" Liza cried in delight.

"She is mighty pretty," Coyote agreed. "Hey, you told me your snowpeople always resembled someone. Who is this one?"

Liza folded her arms and studied the zany snowlady. She looked like someone familiar. But who was it? Then it hit her. She knew exactly who the snow lady looked like. But did she dare tell Coyote? What would he think?

"Do you want to know the truth?" she asked. This was a gamble, but maybe she could trust him. For some reason, after today, she felt like she could.

"Sure."

"She's me as a kid. Fat, with crazy red hair and a sort of garish way of dressing. And a big mouth."

"I haven't heard her say anything," Coyote teased gently.

"Oh, she has a big mouth," Liza said confidently. "Just look at her. You know she does."

"Yeah, I think she probably does."

There, thought Liza. *I've said it.* Would he see her in a new light—forevermore the twerpy fat kid? Had she ruined everything?

Coyote looked her over as if he were trying to envision her the way she'd been. "So, you were a geeky kid, huh? I'd never have known it," he said finally.

"You wouldn't?" Liza asked, pleased.

"Naw. Now me—I was the geek kid of all time. Bowlegged and super-skinny. That's why I started playing guitar, so I would stand out. When I played guitar, I was cool, ya know. Nobody put me down, not even pretty girls like you."

Pretty girls like her. Liza had never been called pretty before. It was wonderful. And how surprising to find that they really were kindred spirits underneath their differences. "I can relate to what you're saying," Liza admitted, taking another gamble but feeling surer of herself this time. "That's why I started acting and doing comedy. Onstage, I feel invincible. In real life, I'm scared to death."

"Scared of what?"

"I don't know. Things. Of not being good enough. Witty enough. Pretty enough. You know. Lovable enough."

He put his hand on her shoulder. It felt warm and comforting. "Yeah. I know how that is," he said seriously.

Who would have believed Coyote Gates would turn out to be someone she could confide in, someone who would understand her insecurities and like her anyway? She felt so close to him as they stood there in the falling snow. It was a great feeling, so unexpected, yet so wonderful.

Liza noticed that people were stopping to look at the snowmen. Most of them were gathered around their snowwoman. It was just like back in Brooklyn. "I think we have a winner," she whispered to him.

"It never pays to be too cocky," he warned.

"Ha!" she snorted. "I can't believe Mr. Cocky of all time is saying that."

"When it comes to snow art I'm not as confident as with music," he explained. "Speaking of music, I hear you guys are having a big wingding for the merchants tonight."

"Boy, everybody knows everything about everybody around here, don't they?" she said.

"It's a small town. Listen, do you have music for entertainment?"

"Not live music," she admitted. "That was kind of my assignment, and I haven't been too successful. You were right—the Razzle Dazzlers were pretty geriatric, and even they didn't want the job."

"How would you like the Lonely Rangers to play?"

"We can't pay," she reminded him.

"That's okay. Think of it as a 'welcome to town' gesture. But we do expect to be fed."

Liza's eyes widened excitedly. "You've got it! Oh, man! This is so great!"

At that moment, a short, stocky man and a tall woman approached them. "We hear this is your snowwoman," the man said.

"Yes," said Liza.

"Well, we're here to give you your fifty-dollar prize payment," he said. Liza looked at the snow-woman. A big yellow ribbon that said "First Prize" was stuck to it.

"Congratulations," said the woman.

When the judges had left, Liza looked up at Coyote. For a moment he looked as stunned as she. Then he threw his hat up in the air and let out a wild howl of happiness.

"We won! We won!" Liza screamed, jumping up and down.

She felt so great! Impulsively, with a soaring heart, she grabbed hold of him and kissed him hard on the mouth. Somewhere, midkiss, she real-ized what she was doing and jumped back. "Sorry," she said.

But his eyes were shining happily. "Don't be sorry. I'm not. I liked it. A lot."

"Me, too," Liza breathed. "I just wasn't sure how you felt about . . . you know . . . me."

"I've liked you right from the start. From the very day I set eyes on you."

"Yeah?" Liza turned away saucily. "I knew that."

"You devil! You did not," he challenged, laughing.

"Did so," she insisted with a teasing smile.

He picked up a handful of snow and tossed it at her. "Did not."

She threw snow back at him. "Did so." In the next instant they were laughing and covering each other with snow. Breathlessly, she fell into his arms, and he kissed her again, long and tenderly.

Sixteen

KC had been so sure she'd be able to track down Jeremy at the Winter Carnival. It was the kind of event that everyone attended. But, after asking everywhere, she'd finally been directed up to the indoor rodeo by a man sitting at the bar in The Hungry Horse. Jeremy was getting ready for the big show tonight.

She had to talk to him about his family. Somehow she needed to get that lift turned back on. He was her best bet. None of the other Towers would listen to her. But he might, and then perhaps he would intercede on her behalf. It was a long shot, but it was the only shot she had.

After parking Kimberly's van in the parking lot, she walked into the rodeo, and was immediately assaulted by the smell of horses and hay. But there was another, more subtle, smell. The pungent smell of people—of sweat and excitement, physical effort and flowing adrenaline—hung in the air.

KC looked at the arena, strewn with a mix of red, white, and blue banners and Christmas wreaths. She tried to imagine the rickety bleachers packed with screaming rodeo fans. Right now she couldn't. The place was too quiet and empty.

Cutting across the dirt riding area in the middle of the circular arena, she headed for a doorway she assumed led to the stables. Maybe someone there could tell her where Jeremy was. She passed the snuffling horses in their stalls. At the end of the stable came the low sound of voices. Hurrying, KC suddenly stopped short.

"There's more money where this came from," a woman was telling a man. "Do right by me tonight and you'll see some of it."

"I have a bull named Blood Foot," he chortled darkly.

"He's a stomper. Even after he gores the rider, he can't leave well enough alone. He likes to throw 'em up and stomp 'em to death just for fun."

"Ohhh, I like that."

Ducking into an empty stall, KC held her breath. She recognized the woman's voice. It was Suzanna's. KC peered through the wooden slabs that separated the stalls. Suzanna was walking out into the center of the barn. Dressed in a trim navy-blue business suit, she was in stark contrast to the burly man she was talking to.

KC was immediately struck with the difference in Suzanna. The banker's whole body language was different. Her modellike posture had melted into a sexy slouch. Even her voice was different— tough and harsh.

"There may even be a ranch overseer's job in this for you, Russ, if all my plans work out the way I hope," Suzanna was saying.

"Oh, yeah?" Russ sneered. "You planning on running the Tower Ranch once you snare that dim-witted Jake Tower?"

Suzanna hooted with derisive laughter. "I'm already running it. Make no mistake about that. I conned the old geezer into giving me total control of the ranch finances. After all, I am a banker."

KC was stunned. Suzanna was so changed. She wasn't the person KC had thought she was at all. How could she have been so taken in?

"A beautiful banker," said Russ. "I guess the old man couldn't believe his good luck. Old Man Tower never could resist a pretty woman."

"Apparently not," said Suzanna. "And that's what's going to get me the Angel Ranch, too."

KC's hand flew to her mouth. What was Suzanna talking about?

"A long time ago some woman sucked the last juices out of his pruny little heart when she dumped him," Suzanna went on. "My grandma knew him back then. She was the maid in the house. She said he went from mean to meaner overnight. My grandma worked in that house until she dropped dead waxing his oak floors. She always said that after Rose Angeletti left him, he was never the same."

"Yeah, I remember hearing something along those lines," said Russ.

"It's true, all right. All it took was that Angel Ranch opening up again to revive his old anger."

"How's that going to get you the Angel Ranch?" Russ asked.

KC crouched forward, anxious not to miss a word.

"That ranch is about to crumble right into my hands any minute," Suzanna boasted. "I've got Grandpa Tower all pumped up on the old feud. I tell him they're building fences on his land and that Mrs. Angeletti is calling him an old fool all over town. The old guy is so proud, he's mortified that everyone is remembering a woman ever dumped him, even if it was a hundred years ago. To him it's like yesterday. Of course, Jake is such a weakling he'll do whatever he's told. So I have him off sabotaging the Angel Ranch at every turn. But I'm the one who's really going to fold it. I've got that Angeletti woman so overextended in loans I'll be able to pick up that ranch for a song once the bank forecloses. There's no way she'll be able to make that balloon payment. Especially now, with the ski lift shut."

KC leaned hard against the wall of the stall. She felt as if Suzanna had just punched her in the stomach.

"Then you'll marry Jake and control two ranches," Russ summed up.

"Oh, I'm not marrying that weasel," Suzanna said with a dismissive wave of her hand. "Why should I do that to myself when I can have it all on my own? I've gotten the Tower finances way overextended, too. Besides that, the old man uses antiquated ranching techniques. He's driving the place into the ground. Jeremy is always after him to update his methods with computers and machines."

"And that's why you want the guy dead?" Russ asked, his voice low.

KC saw a faraway look come over Suzanna's face. "Jeremy is in my way, that's all," she said.

"Didn't you two have a thing for a while?" Russ asked.

"A short while," Suzanna replied. "When I hatched this plan, I went after Jeremy first. I probably wouldn't have minded being married to him. But it's better with Jake. He's more malleable."

"Oh, so Jeremy Tower didn't fall for that sweet smile. That's the real reason he's going to be riding Blood Foot tonight, isn't it?" Russ chuckled. "Women! It's always the same thing with them."

"Shut up, Russ!" Suzanna snapped venomously. "You and I have known each other a long time. Don't let me down on this. You've been paid good money for it. And I don't forget when people do me wrong."

Russ shrugged. "Some rider was going to draw that bull eventually, one way or another. It's no skin off my back if it's Jeremy Tower. I never had no use for the Towers, anyway. That Jeremy don't know what he's getting into with bull riding. It's not like bronc bustin'. That takes skill. This just takes guts. All bulls get crazy when a rider tries to climb on. It don't take Blood Foot to do a number on a rider. First-time riders always get clobbered. They just don't know how really dangerous it is. If you ask me, all bull riders are nuts. You have to be to get up on that animal."

"But Blood Foot will make things that much tougher."

Russ laughed darkly. "Oh, yes, ma'am. Blood Foot will make it near impossible to stay on, and once he's thrown, that bull gores just for fun. That is the meanest bull on earth."

"Good," said Suzanna. Alluringly, she sidled up to Russ. "I just thought of something." She took an envelope from her purse and handed him more money. "Here's another two thousand. Make sure none of the rodeo hands help Jeremy if he goes down."

"Oh, he'll get thrown, all right," Russ assured her. "It's just a matter of how far, how fast, and how cleanly."

Suzanna ran her finger along his jawline. "I know I can count on you."

"Yeah," the man said, eyeing Suzanna hungrily. "You can count on me."

They walked out together. Slumped into the wall, KC watched them leave. Her head was reeling. Suzanna was behind all the disasters! In a million years KC would never have suspected it. But it made sense, perfect sense.

With a pounding heart, KC stood straight and considered her next move. She had to tell her mother what she'd learned. But now, the most important thing was to find Jeremy. His life was at stake.

KC figured Suzanna and Russ had had enough

time to leave. She hurried out of the rodeo and to the van. The snow had stoppped falling, but the traffic leading into town was still slow. Should she drive right up to the Tower ranch and look for Jeremy? No, her chances of finding him were probably better in town.

She started into town and after an agonizingly slow crawl she eventually got into the downtown area. Parking was impossible, so she jumped the van onto a curb on the far side of the village green. She ran across the field of giant snowmen until she came to the main street. Across the crowded street, she saw Suzanna double-park in front of the bank and run inside. KC wasn't sure if Suzanna had done anything technically illegal, but there had to be a way to nail her for wrongdoing.

While she looked at the bank window, thinking what to do, KC saw Winnie walk along, pushing a wheelbarrow. She remembered the cleanup committee. Poor Winnie! KC had envisioned cleanup as pulling down streamers and disposing of paper tablecloths, not pushing a wheelbarrow around the snowy streets.

"Winnie!" KC called, weaving across the crowded street.

Winnie looked up at her and then looked away, hurrying down the street. "Winnie, wait!" KC called, running after her.

"What have I done wrong now?" Winnie snarled when KC caught up with her. "I'm here cleaning up." With the handle of her shovel, Winnie gestured into the wheelbarrow, which was loaded with horse manure. "Shoveling you-know-what," Winnie announced angrily. "That was the job they assigned me. Cleaning up the footpaths so others don't soil their shoes in horse dung. Pretty appropriate, if you ask me. If this was a story in English Lit 101, I think we'd have to say it was symbolic—or is it emblematic?—of the theme of this vacation. Winnie being dumped on to the bitter end."

"Winnie, look, I'm really sorry that you feel that way. I really am. And I'd like to talk about it," KC said.

"You would?" Winnie asked, softening a little.

"Yeah, but I can't now. I have to find Jeremy. I found out something you won't believe. Suzanna is behind all the trouble we've been having."

"Jake's fiancée?" Winnie asked incredulously. "I just saw her get out of her jeep and go into the bank."

"Yeah, I saw her too. She's probably writing up the foreclosure papers for my mother's ranch right now. And not only that, she's trying to get Jeremy killed at the rodeo tonight."

"What?" Winnie shrieked.

"I don't have time to explain any more. Have you seen Jeremy today?"

"As a matter of fact, I did. He even asked me if I knew where you were—which I didn't. He said he was going to go shoot pool at some place out of town called The Mountain Ridge."

"Great! That's great!" said KC, already heading back across the street. "Thanks." She turned and raced through the crowd. If she could catch up with him, maybe there was still time to save his life.

Winnie watched KC disappear into the sea of people.

"I want to talk, but I can't right now," Winnie mimicked KC. She was angrier then ever. All KC had wanted was information. As long as Winnie could be helpful, serve some purpose, she was okay. But when she goofed up or needed some understanding, then she was just Winnie the flake.

"Oh, there you are," a voice called to her. It was a fat woman in overalls and a thick sweater. "What are you doing over here? You're supposed to be clearing the footpaths. Snow is covering the manure and people are stepping into it. They're tracking it into the stores and restaurants. It's a disaster. You should be there cleaning it up."

A local headline formed in Winnie's head. "Towerton Covered in Horse Dung. Winnie Gottlieb to Blame!"

"I was looking for somewhere to dump this," Winnie explained to the woman.

"Why, that's only half full!" the woman exclaimed. "Come see me when it's full." With that she scurried off down the street, her wide rear end waddling behind her.

Winnie began to push the wheelbarrow again, but it was heavy and it stunk. The front wheel bumped on the curb. "Oh, to hell with this!" Winnie cried angrily. "What am I doing this for?"

She abandoned the wheelbarrow and started to walk away, but then she came up with a better plan. Let someone else get dumped on for a change. Someone who really deserved it. And who could possibly deserve it more than Suzanna?

No one that Winnie could think of.

Grabbing the wheelbarrow, she weaved her way over to Suzanna's jeep and opened the unlocked front door. Then with quick motions she shoveled the contents of her wheelbarrow onto the seats.

A wonderful feeling of satisfaction flooded her when she was done. She hadn't felt as good in days.

Above her, the sky began to drop fat snowflakes once again. Jingling the keys to Casper's car in her pocket, Winnie headed toward it. She couldn't wait to get to the bus stop and out of town.

Seventeen

The van slid on the icy road as KC tried to steer around the hairpin turns. She checked the directions she'd received at the gas station, but it was hard to read and drive at the same time. It was beginning to look as if she'd come up an icy mountain in the middle of a snowstorm on a wild-goose chase. She couldn't imagine where she'd made a wrong turn, though.

KC was torn between going forward and turning back. If she didn't go back now, she might not be able to get down the mountain at all. Yet, perhaps the Mountain Ridge was just around the next turn. Snow was accumulating under the wipers, and KC was finding it harder and harder to keep the van on the road. One bad slide would send her careening off the steep cliff ledge.

Finally, as she made a turn, a tall chalet came into view. A sign stood in front of it. KC had reached the Mountain Ridge. She pulled into the nearly empty lot and hurried inside. "Do you have a pool room?" she asked the waiter who came over to greet her.

"Upstairs," the man said.

KC climbed the white pinewood stairs to the open loft overhead. There she saw Jeremy all alone, bent over a pool table, his cue in his hand. Behind him, the entire wall was glass all the way up to the peaked roof. The steadily falling snow made an unreal backdrop.

She waited until he sunk the ball before speaking. "I'm glad I found you," she said.

He looked up sharply, confusion and pleasure mixing in his blue eyes. "Hi. I'm glad you found me, too. I have a burning question to ask you."

"What's that?"

"What does KC stand for?"

KC looked away. She hated the name her parents had given her in their hippie days. But she had no time to be coy. "Kahia Cayanne," she confessed. "Jeremy, I have something to tell you, and it's very important. It's about Suzanna and—"

"Kahia Cayanne," Jeremy echoed. "What a beautiful name. It suits you much better than KC. From now on I'm calling you Kahia Cayanne."

KC was determined not to be distracted. "Jeremy, Suzanna has paid someone to make sure you get the worst bull around. I heard her talking to some guy named Russ. He's going to put you on Blood Foot. She also paid him to make sure no one helps you if the bull tries to stomp on you. I heard them talking myself."

Jeremy frowned and put down his cue stick. "Russ wouldn't do that. He's always had the hots for Suzanna, but still . . . Besides, Suzanna doesn't have that kind of money."

"I'm not making this up," KC cried, on the edge of hysteria. "Suzanna's trying to ruin my mother and your grandfather, too. Please! You can't ride tonight."

Jeremy walked around to the front of the pool table so that he faced her. He propped himself against the table, and with a thoughtful expression, stuck his hands in his jeans pocket. "Are you sure you heard right? I thought Blood Foot was down in Texas, at the Sweetwater rodeo."

"I'm absolutely sure I got it right. Maybe Russ had him shipped up here special for you. Don't be so trusting. Don't be so careless with your life?" she screamed at him. "What are you trying to prove?"

"Hey, calm down." Jeremy glanced toward the stairs. "Look, you don't have to worry. I'm going to be fine. I'm a good rider. And I've watched guys ride bulls dozens of times. I've talked to the best of them. They've told me everything they know. Hell, I'm an ace on a mechanical bull."

"A mechanical bull doesn't gore you once you're down. A mechanical bull isn't Blood Foot. Suzanna wants you killed, Jeremy! She wants you out of the way so she can get her hands on your grandfather's ranch."

His face clouded over. "I know that she's a greedy little monster. She grew up dirt-poor. Her mother and grandmother were both maids in Grandpa's house. She hates me because I see what she really is. But she's not a murderer."

"If you think that, then you don't see anything," KC objected.

"Kahia Cayanne, huh," he said, coming toward her.

"Don't!" KC yelled, pounding the end of the pool table. "Don't change the subject. Don't turn this into a joke."

He threw up his arms in confusion and frustration. "I have to ride tonight. I can't just not ride because I think my bull is too tough. I might as well not show my face in these parts if I do that."

"You might not have a face to show if you *do*

ride," KC insisted.

He reached out and took her hand. "Look," he said. "In bull riding they have a thing they call 'try.' It's what a bull rider has got to have. It's a combination of guts, courage, and a fierce desire to hang on until that ten-second buzzer rings. I want to know if I have try. I've got to find out. It's important to me. Can you understand that?"

KC laughed bitterly. "I'll make sure they put that on your gravestone. *He tried.*"

Jeremy went to the jukebox in the corner of the room and selected a country song. "I've got to," he said quietly, as he looked at the list of songs. "Even if I wanted to, I don't see how I could back out now."

"You're crazy!" KC shouted. Not knowing what else to do, she ran down the stairs and out into the parking lot. *To hell with him,* she raged as she climbed into the van. She'd done all she could. She'd thought he was the perfect man, but he was just like the rest, filled with weird ideas about what it meant to be a *real* man. Ideas that were always completely off the mark, that had nothing to do with the world, at least not the world she knew.

Leaning over the steering wheel, she began to sob. Jeremy's bravery and strength were a big part of what drew her to him, but it was what was going to kill him.

She wiped her eyes and pulled out of the lot.

The snow was falling heavier than ever. What was she doing on a slippery mountain chasing a rodeo rider with a death wish? She'd already spent too much time on him. The big dinner was tonight. She owed it to her mother to be at the ranch right now.

Tears flooded her eyes once again. She wiped them away quickly. She couldn't afford to have her vision blurred. The road ahead was too tricky.

Gently Kimberly put the phone receiver back in the cradle. "Oh, this is a disaster," she groaned.

"Another cancellation?" Faith asked.

Kimberly nodded. "The last six were because of the snow, but this one was a little different. The woman who owns the feed store said that Suzanna told her that Winnie dumped a load of horse manure in the front seat of Suzanna's jeep. The woman and her husband said they weren't coming because Suzanna is her friend."

"First she calls Alec Brady and now she does this. I think Winnie has finally flipped," said Faith with a deep sigh.

The phone rang again. "Want me to take this

one?" asked Casper, coming down the stairs.

"Would you?" Kimberly replied. "I can't face it."

"Angel Dude Ranch," Casper answered the phone. "Oh, gee, um . . . I'm not sure why she did that. I'm sure Mrs. A. doesn't know anything about it. Gee . . . we really would love it if you changed your mind and came. Please don't hold that against us. And don't worry about the snow. If you need to stay over, we have the room. Mrs. A. will gladly put you up if the roads get bad. Well, sure, sure. We understand. Thanks for calling."

"Nice try," said Kimberly glumly.

"Cross off the Hardwoods from the saddle shop," said Casper. "Apparently Winnie—"

"We know. We know," Faith cut him off. "I hope you're hungry, Casper. There's going to be a lot of leftover food tonight."

Just then, KC burst in the front door, brushing heavy snow from her hair. "Anyone seen my mother?" she asked anxiously.

"A big box of brochures was dropped off, so she drove into town to drop them at the Winter Carnival tourist booth," Kimberly explained. "KC, are you okay? You look pretty upset."

Talking in a rush, KC told them everything that had happened. "Geez, Louise!" cried Liza, coming in from the dining room. "I just heard the end of that story. It's unbelievable. It explains a lot, though."

"That's for sure," KC agreed.

"I'd like to stay and talk more, but I have to run," said Liza. "I have to get over to Coyote's place. Can I borrow the van?"

"Sure," said Kimberly.

KC threw her the keys. "The roads are horrible, so drive slow."

"I will," Liza sang out as she hurried out the door.

"At least she's happy," said Kimberly. "She's right, too. The story about Suzanna explains what's been going on around here."

"It might explain why Winnie did what she did, too," said Faith.

"Did you tell Winnie all this?" Kimberly asked KC.

"Yeah. Why?" KC replied.

"Winnie dumped horse dung in Suzanna's jeep," Casper told her.

"All right!" KC cheered. "That's great!"

"Not *so* great," said Kimberly, reluctant to wipe even a fleeting smile from KC's face. "A lot of the merchants are canceling because of it."

"Eight couples, so far," Faith reported sadly. "Six on account of the weather and two on account of Winnie."

"That's almost everyone," KC gasped. "That

leaves only two more couples."

"You won't have to worry about being short-handed now," said Kimberly. "Faith and I could cover serving four people by ourselves."

"Hey, I could do that even with one hand in a sling," Casper joked, in an attempt to lighten the mood.

"That's *if* the other two couples don't cancel," said KC. "And I have a sick feeling we'll be hearing from them." She wrung her hands, and Kimberly thought she might cry at any moment. "This is the end," she said in a choked voice. "This was our last hope of saving the ranch, and now it's buried under a ton of snow." She laughed bitterly. "We all wanted snow so badly. Well, we got it—at the worst possible time."

KC slumped into a straight-back chair beside the Christmas tree. Her long dark hair formed a veil across her face.

"How did it go with Jeremy?" Kimberly asked softly.

"He wouldn't listen to me," KC muttered.

At the desk, the phone rang again. Faith picked it up, and from her expression, Kimberly could tell it was another cancellation.

KC covered her face with her hands. "He's going to ride that bull tonight?" Kimberly asked.

Looking up, KC pushed back her hair. Her eyes

were wet and red. "There was nothing I could say to stop him," she said. "He's going to be killed or crippled."

"You really care about him, don't you," Kimberly observed.

KC began crying even harder. "I don't know why," she sobbed. "But I do."

Kimberly glanced quickly at Casper, who sat on the stairs reading over some typed pages from his paper. "I know what you mean," she said to KC. Why she felt as she did about Casper was a mystery to her as well, but since their escape from the ski lift, she'd become very attached to him. He was suddenly very important to her.

Abruptly, KC got to her feet. "I have to stop him. I don't care what it takes. Even if it means I have to pull the fire alarm in that rodeo this evening, I'm going to keep him from riding a mad bull."

Kimberly looked into KC's wild eyes and barely recognized the cool, collected person she'd come to know. This was a driven, passionately determined person. Instinctively, Kimberly realized there would be no stopping her.

"Oh, no!" KC cried. "Liza just took the van. Mom's got the pickup, and Winnie took Casper's car. What am I going to do?"

"Wait for your mom," Kimberly suggested.

KC went to the window and watched the snow that now fell so heavily it blurred everything else. When Kimberly joined her she felt as if she were staring outside through a piece of shimmering, heavy, white gauze. "What if she doesn't make it home? Or doesn't get here until late? I can't just sit here and wait, wondering every moment if Jeremy is dead or alive. I've got to get there."

Kimberly considered the problem. "It wouldn't be smart to take a horse out in this weather. There are two pairs of cross-country skis in the shed. It's insane . . . but . . ."

KC jumped on the idea. "If I leave now, I can get there in time for the rodeo." She ran for the door.

"Wait!" Kimberly called. "I'll go with you."

"You don't have to."

"Of course I do. You can't go by yourself." Kimberly turned to Faith. "Can you hold down the fort here if that couple shows up?"

"I think I can handle it," Faith said as she walked toward the dining room. "The food is ready to cook, and I have the one-armed wonder here for assistance if I need it."

"Great," said Kimberly, smiling at Casper on the steps. "Just let me go upstairs for my parka, KC, and I'll be right with you."

"Okay, I'll meet you at the shed," KC replied,

pulling open the front door and stepping out into the blizzard.

"Excuse me," Kimberly said as she passed Casper on the stairs. As she went by, she ruffled his sandy hair playfully.

He looked up from his reading and grabbed her leg. "Hang on. I don't think either of you should go out."

Kimberly sat beside him. "KC's going whether I go with her or not," she explained. "So I have to go with her."

Casper got to his feet. "Then I'll go with you, too."

"There are only two pair of cross-country skis. And—no offense—but with that arm, you'd hold us up."

He ran his hand along her arm. "That makes sense, but I don't want anything to happen to you. I care too much about you."

Kimberly smiled at him warmly. "I'll be fine." She got up and went to her room. It felt so good being around Casper, she thought as she grabbed the parka from her closet. When he said he cared about her, she really believed him. She wondered what would happen once they left the ranch, but somehow she wasn't worried. She had a feeling that their new relationship could withstand being a long-distance one. Maybe Casper would consider going to grad school somewhere closer to the University of Springfield. She decided to suggest it, hen the time was right.

On her way down the hall, she was stopped by the odd click and clatter of the fax machine in Casper's room. Running in to the open room to grab the message for him, she couldn't resist the urge to sneak a peek.

What she saw stopped her cold. The identifying information indicated that the fax was coming from a magazine called *The Easterner*. Kimberly had read it a number of times. It was a witty, very sophisticated conglomeration of short stories, book and movie reviews, and travel pieces. It was one of the most prestigious magazines in the country. And it appeared that Casper was going to have an article published in it. What she held was a corrected draft of an article called. "Vacation on the Far Side," by Casper Reilly. It was a review of the Angel Ranch.

So that was his secret. Kimberly had never stopped suspecting that there was something Casper wasn't telling her. He was a reviewer.

What luck! This would change everything. Casper's review was sure to be glowing. People would flock in from everywhere once they read it. A smile spread across her face. She couldn't wait to tell KC. This was such a wonderful, unexpected turn. Just when things looked their bleakest, the sun was about to shine.

As the pages spewed out of the fax, Kimberly raced through the article. *My first clue that things were not intending to go my way should have come when my Rent-a-Wreck failed me before I even entered the far-from-pearly gates of the Angel Dude Ranch. Yet, nothing could have truly prepared me for the chaos I was to encounter within.*

What? This wasn't what Kimberly had expected. She read on as he lampooned everything about the place: the food; the service; even the killer ski lift came under attack. It was all well-written. Casper had a stinging wit she wouldn't have suspected. It was even all true. But it would be the final nail in the Angel Ranch coffin. Casper had to know that. Obviously he didn't care.

"That rat!" Kimberly fumed. How could he do this? He knew how hard Kimberly was working, along with the others, to make the ranch a success. How could he be eating with them, smiling at them, pretending to be on their side, and then every night go up to his room and write the most damning article imaginable? He made the ranch look ridiculous. Was he secretly laughing at them all along? Was his relationship with her just a joke, an amusement to him?

Clutching the papers, Kimberly banged out of the

room and down the stairs. "These are for you," she announced, dropping the papers in a shower around Casper's head. She made a point of stepping on the sheets as she continued down the stairs.

From the corner of her eye she saw him pale as he picked up a sheet and slowly realized what it was. "Kimberly, don't be mad," Casper called, hurrying after her. "I was sent here to write a review, and I wrote an honest one."

Kimberly whirled around and glared at him. "So that's your big term paper."

"I couldn't tell you the truth, or I wouldn't have gotten an objective picture of the ranch. I'd have been given the royal treatment, and that wouldn't have been legit. Don't you see? This is important to me. It's an amazing feat for a college student to get anything published in *The Easterner*. But they loved my idea of reviewing a dude ranch. You know, the Wild West seen from an eastern point of view. It'll make my career."

"And destroy Mrs. Angeletti's." That was probably what galled her most—the fact that he just didn't care what this review would do to the ranch.

"That's not my fault," he insisted quietly. "What if I wrote a glowing review and people came only to find this disaster? No one would ever ask me to review anything again."

"Casper, have you been having a good time?"

"Yes! A great time," he replied.

"I don't see that in your article. Nor do I see anything about how friendly Mrs. Angeletti and everyone has been to you. And I don't see any mention of the fact that Mrs. A. plans to make improvements, or how beautiful the countryside is. All I see is some college kid trying to prove his snotty—or do you prefer the word acerbic—wit. It's easy to be negative, Casper. And I don't like negative people, especially ones who betray trust and try to hurt my friends."

Kimberly turned to leave, but Casper grabbed her arm. "Kimberly, it's not the way you think. This was just a first draft. I was going to make changes."

She could barely stand to look at him. "Well, I'm making changes, too," Kimberly shouted, wrenching away. "My first change is to stop speaking to you. So, good-bye. I have a real friend who needs me right now. And let me just say before I go, I hope you take your review and your career and choke on them!"

Eighteen

L iza was working hard at not smiling too much. She felt it puffed her cheeks and made her look alarmingly like a chipmunk. She'd noted this unattractive tendency in photos all too often. It was hard not to smile, though, when things were turning out so great. Here she was alone with Coyote—the two of them crazy about each other—and about to return to the ranch in triumph with the Lonely Rangers in tow. As soon as Coyote could pull together the best guitars and amps for the gig, they'd return in Kimberly's van. The rest of the band would show up a half hour before the dinner to help set up.

Coyote put one arm around Liza's waist as he pulled a guitar off a hook with the other hand. She looked up at him and tried to read his expression. It wasn't hard to do. His eyes seemed to sparkle when he looked at her. Liza locked her hands around his neck and pulled him to her for a kiss.

Normally, Liza would have been too insecure to kiss a guy first, but it was strangely different with Coyote. Every time she dared to relax and be herself, her bravery was rewarded with his appreciation and understanding.

Still holding his guitar, Coyote enfolded her in his arms. Their kiss was long and breathless. Liza never wanted it to end. "Ohhhh, you are too adorable for words," she cooed at him when they came up for air.

"I'm not the adorable one," he said, his eyes smiling into hers.

Liza rubbed her cheek on his shoulder. So this was what all the fuss was about, all the fuss about love. Liza had never really experienced it firsthand. Sure, she'd had a zillion crushes. She'd even been chased by a few unthinkable geeks. But having the attraction and being the object of a guy's attraction—those two things had never come together for her. Until now.

"I hate to leave you even for a minute, but I

have to go find some amplifiers in the back," he told her. "How big is the space we'll be in?"

Liza scrunched her mouth thoughtfully as she surveyed Coyote's log cabin living room. "The Lazy Q is probably twice the size of this room," she figured.

"How high is the ceiling?" he asked.

She looked up at the peaked ceiling with the loft bedroom jutting halfway out into the living room. "It's what this would be if it had a regular ceiling," she told him.

"Okay, I know what I need," he said. "Be right back."

"Don't be long." She settled into the red corduroy couch in front of the blazing fieldstone fireplace. The fire threw wavering shadows along the wall of the dimly lit room. It was like being the heroine in a movie—a love story.

A pang of guilt hit her. Did she have the right to be this happy when the Angel Ranch was under attack? The situation with Suzanna was serious. Jeremy could be killed, and Mrs. Angeletti might lose everything.

She was doing her bit, though. She'd landed the most popular band in the area to play at the dinner. What more could they ask of her? She was certainly contributing. It wasn't her fault if she was having a fabulous time doing it. It didn't make the contribution any less. Did it?

Coyote returned with the amplifier and stood behind the couch. "You look so great lying there," he said. He kicked his legs up onto the back of the couch and tumbled down lightly on top of her.

Liza giggled and kissed him, small kisses all over his face. He closed his eyes and sighed happily. Liza ran her fingers through his slightly coarse hair. "Don't stop," he murmured blissfully.

"I think you were a golden retriever in another life," she teased gently. "That's what you remind me of: big and handsome and frisky, with lots of thick reddish hair."

"Are you calling me a mangy dog?" He laughed as she continued to stroke his hair.

"Not mangy!" she protested as he slowly got up. "The best dog anyone could have. I love dogs."

They sat smiling at each other for a moment longer, then they got up. Coyote assembled the last of his things and soon they were ready to leave. "Liza," Coyote said as he pulled on his olive-green parka. "What is it that a sophisticated girl like you sees in a guy like me, anyway?"

The question took Liza aback. If anything, she wondered what a gorgeous guy like Coyote saw in her. "I don't know," she replied. "It's one of those chemistry things, I guess. You know, at first I thought I didn't like you at all, but then everything changed."

"Well, when did it change? Did it happen for you the moment we met at The Hungry Horse? Or was it later, at the Towers' barn dance?" he probed.

"What does it matter?" Liza asked. She wasn't sure she wanted to admit that she only liked him initially because he liked her first. It didn't seem the most flattering thing to say, and things were going so well. Why spoil them?

Coyote zipped his coat and looked slightly embarrassed. "I know it sounds like I'm fishing for a compliment, but honestly I'm not. It's just that you didn't like me and then you did. I've been wondering why you changed your mind, is all."

"When did you first know you liked me?" Liza threw the question back at him cagily. "You tell me first."

A look of hesitation flew across his face, but he seemed to push it aside. "The honest truth is, I didn't realize how attracted I was to you until I found out how much you liked me. But . . . but . . . don't get me wrong. I liked you, I just had to be woken up to that fact, is all. When I heard you were so interested in me, that woke me up to what I'd been feeling all along."

"What?" Liza shrieked. "Who told you I liked you?"

"I overheard your friends talking about how you were so in love with me. It was at the Towers' barn dance."

"Which friends?"

"The black gal and the blonde. I forget their names."

"That's impossible," said Liza, anger rising inside her. I never told my friends, or anyone, that I liked you. Kimberly and Faith were the ones who told me how much you liked me. Didn't you tell Casper that?"

His dark eyes narrowed in confusion. "Who?"

"Casper! You never spoke to that blond guy with glasses in the liquor store? You asked him about me, didn't you?"

"I don't drink. My dad was alcoholic, so I swore I'd never touch the stuff. I've never set foot in a liquor store in my life."

Liza's brain whirred into high gear. What, exactly, did all this mean? He claimed to have overheard Kimberly and Faith say she liked him. And she had definitely been told he liked her. Yet he'd never met Casper.

So he liked her because he thought she liked him. And she liked him because she thought he liked her. But both of them had really detested each other.

The sickening truth hit Liza. Kimberly and

Faith had set her up. They'd lied to her—made a fool of her.

She chuckled grimly. "What's so funny?" he asked.

"It's all a bad joke. Let me get this straight. You only liked me because you thought I liked you. Which was a lie. I never liked you. I thought you were a conceited hick. I only liked you because they lied and told me you were crazy about me."

"This is rich," Coyote said, looking away. "Because I never said that. In fact, I thought you were a brash, nervy city girl. And talk about conceited. No one could match you!"

"*I'm* conceited?" she gasped. "That's a laugh, coming from you, the conceit king."

"Hey, I'm not the one with the fancy Hollywood friend and the big connections," he countered. "And at least I'm proud of real things, like my talent. You're boasting about a broken-down old dude ranch that's about to go bust, and I have yet to see these Hollywood friends. I think you're just a liar, lady."

"How dare you call me a liar!"

"I call 'em as I see 'em," he insisted sullenly.

"So do I," yelled Liza. "And I'm calling this quits." Grabbing her jacket, she stomped out of the cabin, slamming the door behind her. The snow swirled around her as she made her way to the van and climbed in. With one hand she brushed away her tears. With the other she turned the key in the ignition.

KC raised her arm to shield herself from the icy, stinging snow. The sun was setting, and KC was chilled to the bone. They'd gone about two and a half miles in their trek toward the rodeo arena, and her legs were sore and her feet ached. "How are you doing?" she asked Kimberly.

"If you don't count the fact that my toes are frozen and I can't feel my nose, I'm fine," Kimberly answered. "I'm sorry. Maybe this wasn't the greatest idea I ever had."

"It's getting me to the arena, that's all I care about," KC assured her. "You look so down, though. I guess you must be regretting this."

"It's not that," said Kimberly as they continued along. "I was just thinking about Casper. Why do men always turn out to be jerks?"

"What happened? You guys seemed happy together." KC noticed Kimberly hesitate, and she worried that she'd asked too personal a question. "If it's none of my business, you don't have to say."

"It's not that," Kimberly replied. "It's that . . .

that . . . Oh, it's really nothing. I'll tell you another time. I don't feel like going into it now."

"All right," KC agreed.

Suddenly, KC's mood brightened. "Look ahead!" she cried. A little more than a half mile up the road, through the dusky light, she could see a line of headlights filing into the rodeo arena. "Come on."

Pushing with their poles, they hurried on. KC forgot her fatigue and aching limbs. In about fifteen more minutes they were mixing with the crowd making its way into the arena. "Warm at last." Kimberly sighed the moment they stepped inside.

KC was carrying her skis on her shoulder. "Would you hang on to these while I go to find Jeremy?" she asked.

"Sure, but what more can you say to him?" Kimberly replied.

"I don't know," KC admitted. "But I can't let him ride. I just can't." She handed Kimberly her skis and poles. "Thanks," she said. It was hard to make her way through the crowd, but her frantic determination made her forget politeness as she weaved and slipped through the crush of bodies. When she got into the main arena the rodeo was already under way. The audience was cheering for a cowboy who was hanging on to a wildly bucking horse.

KC looked around desperately. No sign of Jeremy. Figuring that he must be in the stable, she ran to the front railing. The other day she'd crossed the empty center of the arena to get to the stable. Now she would have to find another way in, preferably the fastest way. When she got to the fence blocking the entry to the stable, she grabbed hold and pulled herself up.

Looking down, she saw a gleaming black bull, waiting to be released from a pen. He snorted up at her and she gasped, unprepared for the size and ferocity of the animal. Its curved horns were larger and sharper than she'd imagined. Most frightening of all were its black eyes. In them she saw anger and menace. This animal knew his own power and potential. He pawed the ground, just waiting to release his energy at the first opportunity.

"Hey!" a rodeo hand called to her. "Get down from there."

He was hurrying toward her. KC knew she had to make a move. Without thinking, she dropped down into the arena and raced around the bull pen into the stable. "Stop! You can't go in there," she heard the man call, but she kept running.

A quick glance over her shoulder told her the man wasn't coming after her. When she looked back she faced a massive black animal. It took a quick second to comprehend that she'd run right into the path of a bucking bronco. She screamed as the horse reared up directly in front of her. Frozen with terror, she knew that in the next second its powerful hooves would land right on top of her.

Suddenly a body came hurtling at her with tremendous impact, smashing into her shoulder. Her breath was knocked out in a whoosh as she felt her feet lift off the ground. Someone had leapt out of nowhere, pushing her out of the horse's path. For a heart-stopping second, KC thought it was Jeremy.

It wasn't.

It was Jake Tower.

He tumbled forward on top of her. Together they fell into a bale of hay. Quickly, he rolled off of her. "What are you? Crazy?" he began to rant. "You could have been—" Suddenly he stopped. "You?" he cried. "What the hell are you doing here?"

KC opened her mouth to speak, but she'd had the wind so completely knocked out of her that she couldn't. She stood and leaned heavily against a stall, bent over gasping for air.

"Is she okay?" asked the cowboy who had been leading out the horse.

"I think so," Jake answered. "I'll stay here and make sure."

"Thanks," said the cowboy as he continued out with the horse.

"You'll get your lungs filled in a minute," said Jake Tower, turning his attention back to KC. There was an unexpected note of concern in his voice.

KC looked up at him, still trying to breathe. For the first time, KC saw the resemblance between Jeremy and Jake. It was in their build, and they had the same square jawline. But, more than that, she'd caught something in Jake's eyes that reminded her of Jeremy.

What was it? Bravery? Idealism? A romantic spirit?

In an instant, though, she was sure Jake didn't realize how he was being manipulated by Suzanna. Though he wasn't innocent, he thought he was doing the right thing. And he was doing it all for love of his grandfather and for Suzanna. What would it do to him when Suzanna dumped him and took his family's ranch?

"Where's Jeremy?" she asked, when she could finally speak.

Before Jake could reply, an announcement blared from the brightly lit arena just outside the shadowy stable. The next event would be the bull riding. "Jeremy Tower will be our first rider tonight." The crowd knew Jeremy and roared its appreciation.

"That answer your question?" said Jake.

"You can't let him ride!" KC cried. "He'll die."

Jake stared at her bitterly. "Jeremy doesn't listen to anything I say. You stop him."

KC ran to the arena in time to see Jeremy burst out of the pen on the back of the bull she'd seen. She was frozen to the spot as she watched Blood Foot bounce insanely on all fours, concentrating every fiber of his being on throwing Jeremy off his back.

The bull was enraged, ferocious. The crowd screamed with excitement. Bright lights illuminated everything, but in KC's mind there was a spotlight trained on Jeremy. He was all she could see, as if she were viewing him through the narrow funnel of a telescope.

His face was calm and serious. As if in slow motion, KC watched him ride with the bull, seeming to meld into his back. She gasped as his black hat flew from his head, but Jeremy didn't even seem to notice.

All the while, KC was counting the seconds. He'd told her a buzzer would sound when the ten-second mark was up. How could a second take so long?

Then, in a flash, time was up. Everything was horrifyingly real as she saw Jeremy lose his grip. Blood Foot tossed him into the air. KC shrieked in horror as he landed hard, making a cloud of dust around him.

"Get up!" she shrieked as the bull focused on him. But Jeremy just lay there. She looked to the cowboys on the side. They were supposed to distract the bull, but they weren't moving. They'd been paid off. They'd taken the bribe.

Slowly, Jeremy climbed to his knees. He took a few wobbly steps and fell down. KC saw that he was dazed. Blood Foot was frenzied with anger. He jumped up, knocking Jeremy back with his powerful hooves.

"Someone help him!" KC screamed. Her scream was drowned out by the cries of the horrified crowd.

Still, no one moved to help him.

The bull jumped again. KC saw a flash of red on Jeremy's leg. It was torn open.

Blood Foot lowered his massive head and pawed the ground. He was going to take his revenge and gore Jeremy with his powerful curved horns.

"No!" KC screamed. She raced into the arena, her feet exploding in her boots. If no one would help him, she would.

Then, with a thud and searing pain, she hit the hard ground. Someone had tackled her. It was Jake Tower. In a flash, he scrambled to his feet and charged out to his brother.

"Yo! Hey!" Jake shouted at Blood Foot as he waved his arms wildly. The bull turned on him, distracted from Jeremy.

At that moment, a cowboy rode out from the stable and ran circles around the bull, drawing him closer to the pen.

Warily, KC moved around them in a broad circle until she reached Jeremy, who was slumped on the ground. A raw, bloody gash on his calf was exposed and dirty under his torn jeans. KC thought she could see the purplish color of his leg muscle. She dropped to her knees beside him.

He winced in pain, his eyes half closed. "I must be seeing things," he said through clenched teeth.

"No, it's me, KC," she said, stroking his sweat-drenched brow.

He closed his eyes, and KC thought he had passed out. Slowly, he opened them again. He gazed up at her, and she forced herself to smile. "It's going to be okay," she said, smoothing his hair.

KC kept her hands on him, instinctively willing her own life force into him. Before this, she'd never believed such a thing was possible, but now she had to try the only thing she could. She saw Blood Foot finally run into his pen and noticed two men running toward her with a stretcher between them. A large puddle of blood was drenching the dirt under Jeremy's leg. His right arm hung at a disturbing angle by his side. KC shut her eyes and concentrated on sending more energy to him. He'd need it.

After what seemed an eternity, the medics reached her and gingerly moved Jeremy onto a stretcher. KC followed them out, holding Jeremy's hand. Soon she was joined by Jake Tower. She and Jake flashed a glance at each other but didn't speak.

The medics took Jeremy through the stable out the side door. In the blinding white storm, the red lights of a waiting ambulance flashed through like a welcome beacon. "I'll ride with him," said Jake as they lifted Jeremy into the back of the ambulance.

"I'll come, too," KC said.

"Go home. I'll be okay, and this storm is getting worse," Jeremy said weakly.

"I don't want to leave you," she insisted.

"Only one person can ride in the back, miss," the medic told her. "I think you should let his brother. If he should pass out, we'll need a relative to sign releases and that sort of thing."

"All right," KC relented, still keeping hold of Jeremy's hand. The thought of leaving him now was torture, but she had to do the right thing for him.

Jeremy squeezed her hand. "So long, Kahia Cayanne."

Nineteen

....

"**D**amn!" Winnie shouted, pounding the phone at the Towerton bus station. Just when she'd finally gotten through to Josh, the line had buzzed and then gone dead. It was probably the storm. She dropped in another quarter and dialed the operator. "I'd like to make another collect call to California," she said, recognizing the operator's voice. "The line keeps conking out."

"Sorry, miss, we're experiencing a lot of difficulty on the lines right now," the operator explained. "I'll put you through to your party again. The number, please."

Winnie gave her the number. The operator's impersonal, polite tone made her feel worse than she already felt. She wanted comfort and warmth on the other end, not some cold robotic voice.

Josh picked up right away. "Yes, I'll accept the charges. Hi, sweetie." That was better, Winnie thought, letting her shoulders relax a little.

"So, what do you think I should do?" she asked him. "My bus is canceled because of the snow, and I can't go back to the ranch. I just can't. Oh! I wish this was *Star Trek* and you could beam me right out of here."

"I wish I could, too, but I can't," he said. "How are the roads there? Can you make it back to the ranch?"

"Probably," Winnie said. "I mean, if I don't hit an ice patch or crash into the abominable snowman or anything like that."

"Could you stay at a hotel until the storm is over?" Josh suggested.

"I don't know where there is one. This isn't exactly a major metropolis." Winnie gazed around at the station with its one bench and its unsettling, greenish neon lights. She was the only one there except for the stone-faced ticket seller and an elderly woman who sat muttering to the inside of her purse. "Oh, God!" Winnie whined into the phone. "I don't want to spend the night in *this* place."

"I think you should go back to the ranch if you can make it safely," Josh said. "I'm sure they'll all be real glad to see you."

"No way," Winnie scoffed. "You don't know how they've been treating me. I mean, you know, because I've told you, but you don't *really* know since you haven't experienced it. Besides, I can't go back now after I made a big deal about leaving. It would be too embarrassing."

"Winnie, they're your friends. You know this is all going to blow over. Why don't you go back and talk to them right now? Get the thing settled instead of letting it brew into an even bigger mess."

"This won't blow over," Winnie insisted petulantly. "This is it, finito, quitsville, the end between me and my so-called best friends."

"Think of it this way," Josh went on. "You can spend the night on a cold bench talking with bus-station weirdos, or you can—"

"How did you know there was a crazy lady here?" Winnie questioned, impressed.

"There always is. Bus stations are a magnet for nuts, no matter where you go. I don't know why. Anyway, you can either stay there and make up with them later, or spare yourself and make up with them now."

"Thank you, Mr. Logic. Why are you so sure

we're going to make up?" Winnie challenged, feeling slightly annoyed at his calmness.

"Because you guys always do make up."

"That's true. But not this time."

"I don't know what else to tell you, Winnie," Josh said, his voice full of frustration. She could almost picture him throwing up his arms and shaking his head, as he always did when he was about to give up on an argument. "I wish I was there to help you. My best advice is to go back. You have to make up your own mind, though."

Winnie sighed deeply. "I can't wait to see you."

"Tell you what, how about if I fly out there for Christmas?"

"Really?" Winnie squealed with delight. Then she frowned. "But I won't be here. But maybe I will be. But I don't think so. Ohhhhh! This is too hard to decide."

"Make your decision and then let me know. If you decide to stay, I'll fly out."

"You're the best," Winnie said. "I'll call you as soon as I decide."

"Okay, let me know."

"Okay, 'bye, I love you," she said as she hung up. Winnie dragged her large bag over to the bench, trying not to look at the old woman. It was hard to ignore her as she continued to rant, her voice growing increasingly loud.

Winnie leaned forward, plunked her chin on her two fists, and attempted to think clearly. She tried to picture how it would be if she returned to the ranch. Would Faith still be furious with her? And what about KC? Would she look down on her for coming back? She had said she wanted to talk. At *her* convenience, of course . . . but, still . . .

Sensing a presence, Winnie looked up to her left. The crazy old woman was staring down at her. She was small with filmy blue eyes and a sharp nose. "So, what's your story?" she demanded imperiously.

Startled, Winnie sat back on the bench. "Huh?"

"Your story?" the woman repeated with irritation. She poked her purse. "Elmore wants to know."

"Elmore?" Winnie asked. "Is . . . is Elmore in your purse?"

"He's one of several, yes," the woman said impatiently.

"Was he your husband?" Winnie questioned.

"Not was. Is!" She snapped open the purse and shoved it at Winnie. There was nothing in it, not even a wallet. "He's mad at me for putting him in there, but I had no choice. It was crowded already, but I had to put him in. He always said he was going to leave me. Then one morning I woke up and he was gone. Never came home, actually. He left because of the others."

"The others?" asked Winnie, not sure she really wanted to hear the answer.

"Sure, the others in my purse. They're all the people who ever bugged me. I put them all in my purse. I thought that would get them away from me, but it didn't."

"It didn't?"

"Nope. Now they talk so much I can't hear myself think. It drives Elmore to distraction. Some nights I can't get their blabbering voices out of my head. And they play little tricks on me. They stop talking and I think they've all run away."

"Isn't that good?" Winnie questioned.

"Nah," the old woman said, waving her hand. "I miss 'em." She trained her filmy blue eyes on Winnie. "So, like I said, what's your story?"

Winnie picked up her bag and stood. "My story is that I have to get going," she said, walking backward and lugging the bag with her.

"There's a storm out there!" the woman cried with alarm. "Are you insane?"

"Probably," Winnie said. "Can I drive you somewhere?"

"I'm waiting for my son," the woman answered, gesturing toward the man behind the counter. "And if he doesn't close this place up soon, he may be the next one to land in my purse."

Winnie looked over to the man, who sat expressionlessly as if he couldn't hear. "All right, then. 'Bye," Winnie said, pushing open the door. She stepped out into the whirling snow. At that moment she realized she was tired, and her arms ached from shoveling horse dung. As much as she didn't want to return to the ranch, it was her only choice. She would simply arrive, go straight to bed, and leave again as soon as the blizzard ended.

Weighted by her bag, she fought her way through the snow to Casper's Rent-a-Wreck. She turned the car engine on and then got out again to wipe off the nearly two inches of snow that had blanketed the car since she parked it. *I don't see why he's always complaining about this car,* she thought, clearing the back window. *It's worked fine for me.*

As she scraped a layer of ice off the windshield with her college I.D. card, she thought about the woman in the bus station. What a funny idea, putting people who bothered you in a purse. Winnie wondered what had happened to the real people. Had she shut them out of her life? Had they rejected her first?

Winnie pictured miniaturized versions of KC, Faith, Kimberly, and Mrs. Angeletti in her purse. At first, the idea made her smile while she scraped. But then a chill ran through her, colder than any freezing wind. That old woman missed her yakking prisoners when they stopped talking. Would Winnie miss her imaginary prisoners if they suddenly disappeared? Yes. Of course she would miss them. Desperately. Especially KC and Faith. They were like a part of her.

With the snow cleared, Winnie got in and turned on the wipers and the lights. For several unnerving minutes, the wheels spun on the ice before she was able to pull out of the spot. The engine grumbled as she forced it through the snow and out of the lot.

The bus station was about three miles outside of downtown Towerton. The road leading to it was long and flat. Not even a gas station's lights illuminated the road. Winnie flipped on her high-beam headlights, but they just made matters worse, reflecting off the falling snow and completely blinding her. Yet the low-beams weren't bright enough.

Winnie felt as if she was moving forward in a small circle of dim light, not knowing what lay ahead in the darkness beyond. It was no way to drive. And outside, the wind howled like phantoms in pain. Cold gusts blasted through the cracks in the old car, making a continual whistle as Winnie drove. Still, Winnie pressed on. After twenty minutes of slow, steady progress, it all started to feel routine. If she kept on like this, it would take a long time, but she would make it back to the ranch in one piece. Thank heavens the car had good heat. It made all the difference.

And then, suddenly the car was sliding on a sheet of ice, turning around in a circle. Winnie spun the wheel this way, then that. In horror, she saw a metal guardrail appear in her headlights. With a sickening crash she banged into it and was ricocheted across the icy road like a ball in a pinball machine. Then, clenching the wheel, she felt the car crash down an embankment, one horrible thud at a time.

When Winnie opened her eyes and got over the happy shock of being still alive and unhurt, it took her a few moments to realize that the worst wasn't over. Pushing open the smashed-in door, she peeked outside and saw that she was in a terrible mess.

She was at the bottom of an embankment, in a blinding, freezing blizzard on a pitch-dark night, and no one was expecting her anywhere. That meant no one would be looking for her.

With a sinking heart, Winnie realized the car was no longer running. She didn't expect to drive it up the hill, but she needed the heat. Ice crystals were already forming on the windshield. Winnie's vivid imagination conjured pictures of the car being completely covered in snow and no one even realizing she was there, frozen inside, until several weeks later when it all melted. With her fingers crossed, she turned the key in the ignition. Nothing.

Winnie slammed the steering wheel and screamed with everything inside her. A primal, bloodcurdling scream. When she was done, she felt a bit calmer.

"Think like Josh," she urged herself. "Be logical."

There was no choice but to start walking. But to where? Towerton or the bus station? The bus station was much closer. From there she could call someone and at least she would be warm.

Putting her shoulder to the door, she climbed out. The snow and wind whipped her face, knocking her hood back onto her shoulders. Getting up the embankment wasn't easy. She slid and fell, finding nothing to pull herself along with. Finally, she struggled up to the road. The bus station wasn't that far away, she told herself.

But then she remembered. The old woman was waiting for her son to lock up the station. Perhaps he'd done it already. Why shouldn't he? There were no more buses coming through. They'd all been canceled.

What if she got there and it was closed?

Winnie pulled her scarf from inside her jacket

and wrapped it around her chin and mouth. Then, ducking her head against the biting snow, she began to walk through the blizzard toward Towerton.

Twenty

*O*h, yes. Yes! KC thought gratefully as a gray pickup truck slowed down on the black, snowy road leading away from the arena. She was numb with cold and her arms and legs felt like lead. Her shoulder ached from where she had landed on the ground when Jake Tower tackled her in the arena, and her scraped face stung in the biting snow. Without the adrenaline rush she'd had when she was trying to get to the arena, the trip home seemed interminable.

Kimberly and KC hurried to the truck. "Where're you gals going?" asked a scrawny young man from behind the steering wheel.

"The Angel Dude Ranch," Kimberly answered.

The man nodded. "I can drop you on Lawder Lane," he said.

"Thanks a million!" said KC. The ranch was right on Lawder Lane.

"Hop in the back," the man told them. "It's not warm, but it's the best I can do." A dark-haired woman smiled at them from the passenger seat. KC would have loved to be in the warm cab, but she couldn't expect the man to throw his wife into the back.

"It's great," Kimberly assured him. "Thanks."

Unhooking their skis, KC and Kimberly climbed into the open pickup. The truck started up again and they were on their way. KC shivered and wrapped her arms around herself. She hadn't realized how the motion of pushing along on the skis had been keeping her warm. Now she was completely frozen, but they'd be home in a fraction of the time, and her throbbing legs appreciated the break.

"I guess Jeremy knows you were telling the truth now," said Kimberly, huddled in a corner of the pickup.

KC nodded. Suzanna hadn't killed him, but who knew how badly hurt Jeremy was. Maybe she had succeeded in getting him out of her way. If he had to spend months recuperating, he wouldn't be in much shape to thwart her plans.

The thought that Suzanna was succeeding in her plans burned inside KC. She wasn't about to stand by and let her mother's dreams crumble into the hands of a greedy viper. No way. She'd been willing to run interference with an enraged bull to help Jeremy, so how much tougher could old man Tower be? She'd talk to him no matter what. "I'm not afraid of anyone," she said.

"Huh?" asked Kimberly, who had been lost in her own thoughts. "Not afraid of whom?"

"Old Man Tower. I'm going to the ranch and tell him what I know about Suzanna. She almost killed Jeremy tonight. Whatever he and Jeremy feel about each other, Jeremy is still his grandson."

"What will you gain by talking to him—besides a very unpleasant experience?" Kimberly asked logically.

KC wasn't sure. But if she could expose Suzanna, then she wouldn't have to fight her all alone. She just couldn't let Suzanna win. "He should know what's been happening," KC insisted. "I'll jump out at the Tower Ranch. You keep going on to Lawder Lane."

"Forget it," Kimberly objected. "You're not going up there alone."

"All right. Thanks," said KC. They sat silently

until they were close to the front gate of the Tower Ranch. KC rapped on the back window of the old truck as it slowly made its way through the blizzard. The man turned questioningly. KC pointed to the gate of the Tower Ranch. "Stop here, please," she shouted through the deafening wind when he rolled down the window.

Slowly he pulled to a stop at the side of the road. "Are you sure you want to do this?" asked Kimberly as they climbed out of the back.

"Absolutely sure," KC confirmed. With their skis slung over their shoulders, they went to the front window. "Thank you very much for the ride."

"You should call someone to come get you from the Tower place when you're done. This is no night to be out skiing. If you can't do that, you should stay over," the man advised.

"We will," KC said, eager to get up to the Towers' house. "Thanks again." She walked off a few steps and then turned back. "Would you mind calling the Angel Dude Ranch and telling them that KC and Kimberly are at the Towers' place. I don't want them to worry."

"Sure, will do," the man promised.

As they drove away, Kimberly snickered. "Yeah, I can just see us as overnight guests at the Tower Ranch."

"Not too likely," KC agreed. Together they began walking up the long road leading to the main house. When they got there, the huge brick house was like a dark mountain standing silently in the snow. It was more of a mansion than a house, with a four-story midsection and a two-story wing on either side. The huge place was dark except for a lamp burning in a room to the right of the wide, carved door.

Kimberly grabbed KC's arm. "Look," she said, pointing to the window.

Through a gauzy white curtain, KC saw Suzanna. She was standing there, talking with great animation to someone KC couldn't see.

"Do you still want to go in?" Kimberly asked.

"More than ever," KC replied. Right now her rage and fury gave her all the nerve she needed to face anyone. Seeing Jeremy carried off on a stretcher and knowing her mother was on the brink of complete ruin had swept her into a state of powerful righteous indignation. She was not going to be stopped.

When they got to the wide, carved door, KC raised her hand to knock, then stopped. To her surprise, she saw that the door was slightly open, as if someone had come through in a great hurry.

Boldly, she pushed in the door and stepped into the front hall. Kimberly lingered cautiously outside the door. "Come on," KC waved her in. There was no time for timidity.

Suzanna's voice wafted out into the hall. Once again, she sounded like Suzanna the kindly banker. The Suzanna KC had witnessed in the stables was well under wraps. "I'm sorry I had to be the one to tell you about Jeremy, Grandpa," she said, oozing concern.

"I begged him not to ride that bull," came the old man's voice, choked with grief.

"I know you did, Grandpa," said Suzanna. "We all begged him. But you know how Jeremy is."

Just then, Jake Tower burst in through the front door. His eyes were wild, and it scared KC. "What are you two doing here?" he demanded of KC and Kimberly.

"How's Jeremy?" KC asked, ignoring his question.

"Worse than we thought," he answered. "Besides his leg wound, he's got a broken arm and a broken rib. The rib punctured his lung. He's not doing good at all."

"Why did you leave him?" KC asked.

"The docs took care of him. Now they want him to rest," said Jake.

At that moment, Suzanna stepped out into the hall. "Jake," she said. "How's Jeremy?"

Jake glowered at his fiancée. "Not great, but

well enough to talk," he said, spitting out the words. "He told me things about you, Suzanna. Did you pay Russ to keep anyone from helping him? And to make sure he drew Blood Foot? Did you?"

"That's a lie!" Suzanna replied instantly. "Where did he hear that?"

Jake pointed at KC. "From her."

"From . . . from . . . you?" Suzanna sputtered.

KC drew a deep breath. She could see Suzanna was going to fight all the way. "I was at the rodeo stable today," KC said. "I heard you bribe Russ to get Jeremy on Blood Foot tonight."

"What?" cried Lewiston Tower, standing in the living-room doorway.

KC knew this was her moment to speak. "There are things you should know, Mr. Tower," she said, looking at the old man. "You too, Jake. Jeremy only knows part of the story."

"Let's not hover here," said Mr. Tower. "Step into the living room."

He stepped back inside, and the others followed. In a rush of words, KC went on to tell everything she'd heard that afternoon in the stable, about how Suzanna was planning to buy up both ranches for a song, and dump Jake once that was done.

As she spoke, the old man turned increasingly

pale, while Jake grew red in the face. "She's nurtured this grudge against my mother and she's been setting the two of you up for a long time now," KC concluded.

"Is all this true?" Jake growled at Suzanna.

With eyes that reminded KC of a caged animal, Suzanna's eyes darted from person to person. She seemed to be weighing her best reaction.

"Well, is it!" Jake screamed at her. KC cringed at the hurt and betrayal in his voice.

"Yes," she said coolly.

KC braced herself for what was to come. She calculated that if Suzanna was willing to reveal the truth, she must be in a strong position.

"Thank goodness you didn't succeed," said Mr. Tower.

"You're wrong. I've already succeeded," Suzanna told him, seeming to pick up strength as she boasted. "You're already sunk too deeply into debt. Maybe if you'd listened to Jeremy, and modernized like he told you to, things might have been harder for me. But as it was, you ran the ranch into the ground yourself. All I did was nudge you along with bad investments and too much debt."

"You told Grandpa not to listen to Jeremy," Jake snarled.

"He didn't have to do what I told him,"

Suzanna said with a mocking shrug. "He was a fool to listen to me."

"I trusted you," Mr. Tower croaked. His ashen color worried KC. She wondered if Suzanna was trying to goad him until he had a heart attack. She could just imagine what Suzanna had cajoled him into putting into his will. It wouldn't be a bit surprising if Suzanna was the executor of everything he owned.

"Who asked you to trust me?" Suzanna yelled, suddenly losing her aloofness. "You're a foolish, cheap old man. I've hated you all my life. My family lived in a crappy little cabin on the edge of your land. Well, when I take over the ranch and move in here, *you* can have the cabin."

"I'll never sell this ranch to you," Mr. Tower said.

"Yes, you will," Suzanna replied smugly. "Because I'll let it be known that it's about to be repossessed by the bank. Then no one will make you an offer, because they'll know they can buy the ranch much cheaper from me. The longer you hang around waiting for a buyer, the closer you get to foreclosure. Your choice will be to accept my offer or lose your ranch and get nothing for it." Suzanna turned to KC. "The same thing goes for your mother. Once she misses that balloon payment—and she will—it'll just be a matter of months."

"Where are you getting the money to be bribing folks and buying ranches?" Jake challenged.

Suzanna smiled at him coyly. "I'm a money manager."

"Embezzler is more like it," KC spoke up.

Suddenly, an unexpected figure appeared in the living-room doorway. "Casper!" Kimberly gasped. He stood there in his jacket, still red-faced from the cold outside. KC tried to read the look on his face. He seemed to be exultant about something. But what? And what was he doing there?

With an ever-widening smile, he triumphantly held up a small portable tape recorder. "I drove up in your mom's four-wheel pickup to get you guys, and I saw the door was open," he said. "I just happened to have this thing stuck in my pocket."

"How long have you been in that hall?" Suzanna demanded.

Casper stepped into the room. "Long enough to record a lot of good stuff for my article," he said blithely.

"What article?" Kimberly asked.

"The one that's going to be published in *The Easterner,*" he said. His eyes met Kimberly's meaningfully. "The one I'm going to substitute for my review of the Angel Dude Ranch."

"Review?" asked KC, confused.

"I was going to tell you, but I figured you had

enough on your mind for tonight," Kimberly explained. "Casper was really at the ranch to review it."

"But I've gotten onto something much better, and I've convinced my editor of it," Casper spoke, beginning to pace around the room excitedly. "This land-fraud deal has everything. Greed, treachery, romance, and betrayal. It's even got cowboys! It's got Pulitizer Prize written all over it. Picture that! Me, not even out of college, and a Pulitizer Prize-winning journalist."

"Slow down, son," said Mr. Tower. "What are you talking about?"

"When KC told me what she'd learned about Suzanna, I saw that it had the makings of a great article, so I proposed it to my editor. She was eager for a scandal story. So, even if Suzanna gets away with her little plan, everyone will know about it. She'll be shunned. Who knows? Maybe even arrested!"

"You have no proof," sneered Suzanna. KC had to hand it to her—the hotter things got, the more aggressive she seemed to become.

"True," Casper admitted, turning toward Suzanna with matching aggression. KC would never have imagined he could be this assertive and bold. "Though I do have an eyewitness to your conversation with the stable guy. Still, it would have been your word against KC's," he continued, advancing until he was standing right in front of her. "But now I have your voice on tape. And I'll be doing some more investigating. You know, talking to people at the rodeo, and your employers at the bank. Maybe they should audit your books, huh? That sort of thing. I'm confident that I'll be able to make a pretty convincing and compelling case against you."

"All right, Mr. Electronics!" KC cheered. She turned to Suzanna. "You might want to consider changing your plans. Maybe Plan B should be to move out of town as fast as possible."

"That's right. Out of my house!" Lewiston Tower thundered. "Now!"

Then she grabbed her coat and stormed from the room.

For a moment, no one spoke. Kimberly and Casper seemed to be carrying on a silent conversation with their eyes, beaming at each other from across the room.

"We should go see about Jeremy," KC said.

"I'll drive you down," Casper offered.

"I can take her," said Jake, looking drained. "Come on, Grandpa. Why don't you come, too?"

The old man looked away. "I don't think Jeremy would be very happy to see me. We spoke some harsh words the last time we talked."

"Then maybe now is the time to set things straight," KC suggested quietly.

Mr. Tower raised his head. For the first time, he looked very old to KC. "Maybe so," he agreed. "Let's go."

Twenty-one

*F*aith drummed her fingertips along the top of the ranch's reception desk and listened to the phone ringing on the other end of the phone wire. Crackles ran along the line, threatening to break the connection between Faith and the Towerton Bus Station. "Come on," Faith muttered. "Somebody pick up." After nearly twenty rings, Faith hung up.

"Any luck?" asked Liza, who sat by the window looking forlornly out at the falling snow.

"No," Faith replied. She took a phone book from the bottom drawer of the desk and looked up the number for the main bus depot in Grand

Falls. Her spirits sunk as she listened to the informational recording which spoke to her when she called. "The Towerton station has been closed for hours," she reported to Liza. "So where could Winnie be? Do you think she'd try to drive to Grand Falls in that old wreck?"

"No, I don't," Liza said. "She knew Casper needed his car back. It wouldn't be like her to do something that inconsiderate."

"You're right," Faith agreed. "Winnie is basically a very good person." She let her head slump into her hands. "God! I feel so guilty!"

"You?" asked Liza, looking away from the window. "What do you have to feel guilty about?"

"The way I jumped all over her about Alec Brady," Faith admitted. "I mean, Winnie was right. He could have been making up the story. I've known her much longer than I've known him. I should have believed her. I was just so upset and embarrassed."

"Well, I have you beat in the guilt department," Liza said slowly.

"What do you mean?" asked Faith.

"I mean I was the one who phoned Alec Brady."

"You!" Faith yelped. "Why?"

"Because getting celebrity guests here is the one thing that might have saved the ranch. You were too proud to call, so I did it for you. I did it for the ranch, that's all."

"Then why did you tell him you were Winnie?"

Liza looked at the wide-planked floor. "I got cold feet at the last minute."

"Yeah, because it was a crummy thing to do and you knew it," Faith said heatedly, getting up from behind the desk. "My relationships are my business, not yours. When are you going to get that through your head?"

"Hah!" Liza hooted disdainfully. "You're a fine one to talk, after what you did."

"Which is what?" Faith asked cautiously.

"You know very well what. The way you set me up with Coyote. That's why I don't feel that I owe you any apology. You've already gotten your revenge. You made a real fool of me and it hurts."

"Now you know how it feels," Faith replied, feeling badly nonetheless. She walked around to where Liza sat. "Besides, you should be thanking Kimberly and me for getting you and Coyote together. Don't you like him?"

Liza threw her arms into the air. "Yes—I *was* wild about him until I found out I'd been tricked into falling for him," she exploded.

"Liza, you liked him right from the start. We could tell. That's what gave us the idea in the first place," Faith explained. "And if he hadn't liked you, he wouldn't have gone for it so easily."

"I don't know," Liza pouted, slumping down in

the chair. "It might be true that I liked him, but now I don't know if he liked me. Maybe it only appealed to his conceited vanity. Or maybe he figured I'd be easy to get in bed—which I would have been if I hadn't realized the truth in time."

Just then, Mrs. Angeletti appeared on the stairs. Faith felt so sorry for her. She'd returned from town only to find her entire dinner snowed out. And, in order to explain why her waiting staff seemed to have deserted her, Faith told Mrs. Angeletti all that KC had learned about Suzanna's plot to ruin her. The news seemed to devastate her. Almost immediately, she'd complained of a splitting headache and disappeared up to her room. "Has Casper returned with KC and Kimberly yet?" she asked Faith.

"Not yet," Faith reported. "But I'm sure they're okay."

"I hope so," Mrs. Angeletti fretted. "I wish they had never gone up there. Who knows what could have happened."

As if on cue, Kimberly and Casper seemed to blow in the front door. Faith thought they looked strangely elated, considering everything that they must have been through. They held hands and smiled.

"Where's KC?" Mrs. Angeletti asked urgently.

"Down at the hospital with Jake and old man

Tower," Kimberly said. "They wanted to see how Jeremy was doing."

"With the Towers?" Liza questioned, getting out of her seat.

Kimberly and Casper filled them in on everything that had happened at the Tower Ranch. Mrs. Angeletti smiled at the part where Suzanna was sent scurrying from the house. "But wait a minute," she questioned when the story was done. "Where is Winnie? I thought she was with the rest of you."

"She wanted to go home," Faith told her. She hadn't told Mrs. Angeletti this, wanting to spare her the extra worry.

"Whatever for?" Mrs. Angeletti cried, raking her hair.

"She felt like everyone was dumping on her," Liza explained. "Her feelings were hurt."

Mrs. Angeletti bit her lip. "I was unkind to her the other day," she said guiltily. "It wasn't fair, but I needed someone to blame for you girls crashing the Tower dance."

"And KC exploded at her about the soup, and I yelled at her for something she said she didn't do," said Faith. "I guess we've all been rough on her."

"Oh, dear, I feel terrible," said Mrs. Angeletti.

"She probably headed for the bus station, but

it's closed," said Faith. "I don't know where she could be."

"And she's driving the least-reliable car known to humankind," added Casper grimly as he pulled off his jacket.

"I'm calling the sheriff," said Faith. If anything happened to Winnie, Faith knew she would blame herself for the rest of her life. She called information for the number of the Towerton police department. When she got through she reported Winnie as missing.

"What did he say?" Kimberly asked when Faith hung up.

"He says he'll send out a search party in forty-eight hours. That's standard procedure."

"Forty-eight hours!" Liza cried. "She could freeze to death in that time."

"You're right," said Mrs. Angeletti as she headed for the front-hall closet and took out her jacket. "I'm going out to look for her in the pickup."

"I'll take my van and look, too," said Kimberly.

"I'll come with you," Casper voluteereed.

"And I'll come with you, Mrs. Angeletti," said Faith.

"No, Faith, somebody had better stay here in case Winnie comes back or calls," Mrs. Angeletti told her. "We'll check in with you from time to time."

"All right," Faith agreed. It would be torture to just sit and wait, but she knew Mrs. Angeletti was right. "Good luck," she said as the others went out the door. Then she buried her face in her hands and prayed. "Please let her be okay," she murmured. "Let Winnie be okay."

"Room two-oh-three is down the hall to your right," the nurse at the Grand Falls hospital told KC. Too anxious to wait for Jake and Mr. Tower, KC hurried ahead. All the aching in her exhausted body was forgotten as she went down the hall. All that mattered was the sight of Jeremy alive.

When she reached the open doorway to his room her blood ran cold.

Jeremy's bed had been stripped.

KC knew what a stripped bed meant—that the patient had died.

Then, as if he were a ghost, Jeremy stepped out of the bathroom. He leaned heavily on a crutch, and a swollen, purplish bruise ran across his right cheekbone.

KC's hand flew to her mouth and she shut her eyes in relief. "Oh, God!" she sighed. "I saw the stripped bed and I thought that . . . that."

"You thought I kicked the bucket?" he asked with a smile.

She opened her eyes and drank in the sight of him in his hospital gown and robe, his long hair caught back in a ponytail. His arm was in a cast up to his shoulder and his leg was splinted and heavily wrapped. Ace bandages peeked out from the top of his hospital gown.

Their eyes met as both of them smiled softly. KC felt as if they had come through some awful storm and were now safely washed ashore. It was a feeling of exhaustion and great happiness.

Jake and Mr. Tower arrived at the room. At the sight of his grandfather, Jeremy's battered face grew cold.

KC tensed as the two men stood facing each other wordlessly.

The old man made the first move. "How are you, Jeremy?"

"I'll live," Jeremy replied.

"Suzanna admitted everything," Jake told his brother. "There's even more to it than you know."

"All of us were fooled by her," said Mr. Tower. "All of us but you."

"Oh? You mean I'm not such a know-nothing, after all?" Jeremy said bitterly.

Mr. Tower put one of his gnarled hands on Jeremy's shoulder. "I've misjudged you, son. Probably because you look and act so much like your father. But you're not him, and I've been hard on you. Even Suzanna admitted I should have listened to what you had to say about running the ranch."

"Is that so?" Jeremy asked warily.

With a cold voice, Jake told Jeremy all about Suzanna's sleazy manipulations.

"If it wasn't for this little lady here," said Mr. Tower nodding toward KC, "we wouldn't have caught onto her until it was too late."

Jeremy looked at KC warmly. "At least you had the horse sense to believe her, Grandfather," he said. "I didn't."

"Guess what we heard on the local station on the way over?" KC said.

"That a local knucklehead almost had his lights put out by a crazed bull because he didn't have what it took?" Jeremy supplied a possibility.

"No," said KC. "That you broke the record for staying on Blood Foot. Nobody's ever stayed on him more than three seconds. You rode him for five and a half."

"No kidding?" said Jeremy, clearly pleased. When KC saw the delight on his face, she almost regretted telling him. It would only encourage him to try again. But it was better than the defeated expression that had been there before.

"Congratulations," said Mr. Tower. "Now

shouldn't you be lying down? What about that punctured lung?"

"Turns out they were wrong," Jeremy explained. "It's bruised, but not punctured."

"Good," said Mr. Tower. "Can you forgive me?"

KC could tell how much it took for the proud old man to say the words.

"Sure. Hey, I haven't been a saint," Jeremy replied.

"None of us has been," Jake mumbled.

KC leaned back against the wall, trying to withdraw from the scene a bit. This was their private moment of reconciliation. She slipped out into the hallway, but glanced back and saw Mr. Tower embrace Jeremy in a hug.

"Everything okay in there?" a nurse asked crisply as she scurried along.

"Everything's great," KC replied. "Great."

Twenty-two

The next morning Winnie sat in a small diner just outside of Towerton. It was long and narrow with lots of stainless steel, faded blue vinyl booths and a shiny blue Christmas tree in the corner. Her idea of heaven it wasn't, but that was fine by Winnie—the less like the afterlife and the more grittily real, the better.

Winnie had found herself thinking a lot about the next life as she had trudged through the snow the night before. She wasn't even sure there was one, but she hoped so. The wind and cold had cut into her so bitterly that she was sure she wasn't long for this life. She didn't know if she was on the right road, or heading in the right direction, or if she would ever be warm again.

But here she was, thanks to the angel who had driven by in a four-wheel-drive jeep, then stopped and backed up for her. The angel who was sitting across the table from her right this minute—a gorgeous guy with dark hair, a great physique, and a terrific smile. A face she was very familiar with, although she barely knew him.

It was Alec Brady.

Winnie thought about the movies she'd seen where people were really dead, only they didn't realize it. It crossed her mind that perhaps that was what had happened to her. After all, how likely was it that she would be lost in a blizzard only to be picked up by a major movie star?

"You have a strange expression on your face. What are you thinking?" Alec asked.

"I was wondering if I was dead," Winnie confessed sheepishly.

Alec laughed. "You look alive to me."

"You're sure I'm not lying in a snowbank somewhere, having a last delirious dream before succumbing to frostbite?"

"I'm sure," he confirmed, leaning back in the booth. "You're sitting in a Towerton diner having breakfast with me. And, as far as I know, I'm not a ghost. Though there were a few moments last night when I thought I might end up that way."

"Tell me about it," Winnie agreed as she sipped the hot tea in front of her. She laughed softly at the memory of the night before. "By the time I saw the headlights of your jeep, I was so cold I couldn't think straight. And then, when you stopped, I was like, 'Oh, it's Alec Brady, of course.' I was too numb to be surprised. But now that my brain has thawed, I'm in a state of shock."

"Well, I was pretty glad to see you, too. I'd been lost on that godforsaken road for two hours. At that point I had no idea where I was going."

"I didn't have a great idea where we were, either," Winnie said.

"But at least you had *some* idea." He laughed. "I was completely lost. And I was exhausted. The minute I heard the Paris location work was postponed 'till January, I jumped on a jet and flew in. But I'd been filming all day, and then I drove around in that rented jeep for so long. I was about to fall asleep at the wheel."

"The sound of my teeth chattering probably kept you awake once you met me. Thank goodness they had two rooms at that motel," said Winnie. "We never would have made it back to the ranch last night."

"Speaking of which, maybe you should call the ranch and tell them you're okay," Alec suggested.

Winnie looked at the clock on the wall. It wasn't even seven yet. "Naw," she disagreed. "They're all asleep. And they're not missing me. They think I left."

"How come you were leaving?"

"Misunderstandings. I had several of them with several people and I got fed up."

"I know how that can be," Alec sympathized.

"Which reminds me. I hope you don't mind my asking this, but did you really get a message from someone telling you Faith wanted you to come here?"

"Yes, from you," he answered with a confused frown.

"It wasn't from me."

"Then who? It was on my machine and the person said she was you," Alec insisted.

"I don't know who called you, but it wasn't me. It wasn't Faith, either. She was totally blown away by it."

"Do you think it was just some joke?" he asked. "Maybe I shouldn't have come."

Winnie was amazed. This was almost more surprising than meeting Alec in the middle of the night in the middle of a blizzard. He was feeling insecure. She didn't know insecurity happened to hunky major movie stars.

"Forget it," said Winnie. "She'll love it that you're here. She just didn't want you to think she was some movie-star chaser or something."

"Faith?" Alec laughed as the waitress put an order of scrambled eggs and bacon in front of him. "Not likely. That's the last thing on earth I would think of Faith. No, she's one of the truly cool people of the world. When I was hanging out with her on the Springfield campus. I felt like I was me, a person. Most of the time I feel that people *want* something. Even the women I date usually wind up wanting a role in my next film or something. With Faith it's not like that."

"Well, that's cool," said Winnie, spreading cream cheese on her bagel. "You should tell her so."

As she spoke, Winnie realized their waitress was hovering near their table. Winnie looked at her and saw the blond woman shifting from foot to foot. Alec followed Winnie's gaze and smiled at the waitress.

"You are Alec Brady!" the woman cried, delighted. "I knew the minute you smiled. I mean, I thought it was you when you walked in, but I just couldn't believe it."

"Hi," Alec said. "We're glad you were open."

"Oh, yeah, we open early for the skiers and the truckers," the waitress explained as if she were in a blissful daze. "Not that there's been much skiing, but now there will be, for sure."

At that moment two men in heavy coats tromped in, stamping snow from their boots. They squinted at Alec and then settled in at the counter. The waitress brought them each coffee. Winnie watched her talk to the men excitedly. From her darting glances, Winnie knew she was telling them Alec Brady was in the diner.

One of the men came to their table and tossed a napkin down. "Would you sign that, please?" he asked gruffly. "It's for my wife. We saw you last week at the movies. She's a big fan."

"Sure thing," Alec complied pleasantly. "You got a pen?"

The waitress scurried over. "I do. And could you sign one for me?"

"No problem. What's your name?"

Winnie saw that the other man had gone over to the pay phone near the cigarette machine. "I'm telling you it *is* him," she heard him say to someone on the other end.

More and more customers were coming into the diner. The word spread and Alec quickly became the focus of everyone's attention. One autograph led to another once people saw that he was more than willing to sign them. Winnie loved it. She felt like a movie star herself.

"It is him!" a dark haired woman in her twenties shouted as she and three of her friends ran into the diner. "It's true."

"This is a bad sign," Alec said, leaning across the

table to whisper to Winnie. "Word is out. It's eat-and-run time." Winnie nodded. She felt very cool being on the inside, escaping the fans in the company of a movie star, instead of being one of the crazed fans chasing down a star.

Another of the four women, a short redhead, approached the table with a camera in her hand. "I'm from *The Towerton Gazette*," she said. "I hate to interrupt your breakfast, but could we do a quick interview?"

"Very quick," Alec agreed hesitantly. Winnie saw his shoulders tense and the easygoing expression begin to fade from his face.

"Sign my autograph first," the woman behind her insisted. "My name is Cindy."

While Alec signed—his quick, jerky motions showing signs that he was losing his patience— Winnie had a brainstorm. She fished a pen from her purse and pulled a napkin from its metal holder. *Tell them you're staying at the Angel Dude Ranch,* she wrote. *Very hot new spot. Lots of stars plan to come. Okay?*

She folded the napkin and slid it across the table to him. He read it and frowned. "Are you sure?" he asked.

"Yes," she said with an emphatic nod.

"So, what brings you to Towerton?" the woman from the *Gazette* asked.

Alec took the opportunity to do just as Winnie asked. He extoled the virtues of the Angel Dude Ranch. Everyone in the diner was glued to his words, and the reporter wrote feverishly. Winnie supressed a smile as he went on and on about a place he'd never even seen. She was so focused on him that she barely realized the diner was becoming jam-packed with people, all of them standing around staring at Alec.

Once Alec stopped talking, the throng of autograph seekers pressed in on him. Thrilling as it was, Winnie was starting to become uncomfortable. It felt as if a human wave was cresting around her, and at any moment, would engulf them both.

Alec seemed to have had the same feeling, because he got up and put two twenties on the table. A moan came from the crowd as he took Winnie's hand and guided her through the mobbed diner toward the door. As they went, people waved papers and pens at him.

"Just one more," they begged. "Alec, please."

Some reached out just to touch him.

With a polished, apologetic smile, Alec waved them way. Watching him in action, Winnie was keenly aware of what a truly big star he was. This wasn't the first time he'd done this. He knew how to handle it—which was good, because the crush of the crowd was beginning to make Winnie nervous.

People followed them out to the snowy parking lot, still reaching out for him and begging for autographs. With a last sweeping wave, Alec got into his jeep, pushing the passenger door open for Winnie. "I love you, Alec," a teenage girl with braces screeched in Winnie's ear as she closed the door.

"Wow!" Winnie said as Alec started the engine. "I always thought it would be great to be mobbed by admiring fans, but now I'm not so sure."

"It gets to be a bit much sometimes," he agreed.

"Yeah, a little scary."

"You get used to it." He drove the jeep slowly through the crowd. "After a while, you get a sense of when to leave. Things can get out of hand if you don't."

Once they were out of the lot and back on the road, Alec realized he still didn't know exactly how to get to the ranch. "Would you mind navigating?" he asked. "Then I'll drive you back to the bus station if you want."

"Okay," said Winnie. "I suppose I should go back and tell Casper about his car." She sighed deeply. "He can join the rest and be mad at me for another Winnie Gottlieb screw-up. But you know what? I don't care. I'm not even mad at them anymore. There's nothing that I can't straighten out. I guess almost dying puts things in perspective."

* * *

Faith sat cross-legged on the floor near the glittering Christmas tree. She is hunched over a length of bright red foil paper, wrapping the Christmas presents she'd picked up at Winter Carnival. No one was around. They were all still out looking for Winnie. Once again Faith had been assigned the job of standing by and waiting for Winnie to call.

Crazy with worry and feeling like a zombie from spending a sleepless night, Faith folded the paper over a handcrafted ceramic mirror she was giving to Kimberly. This year everyone was getting ceramic gifts from her, since she'd fallen in love with the work of a particular local artist.

When she finished wrapping the mirror, she picked up the small white box which held Winnie's gift. Angry as she had been that day, she would never *not* get Winnie a present. Inside were earrings she knew Winnie would adore. Each earring was a spray of tiny, shimmering stars dangling from delicate gold cords attached to a ceramic moon clasp. The stars were glazed in iridescent colors and varied in size.

Faith opened the box and held the delicate pieces in her hand. They would look great on Winnie. They were just like her—a little offbeat, but lovely just the same. Faith dropped them back into their cotton-lined box and wondered if she should wrap them. Would Winnie be there to receive them?

Pushing that thought from her head, Faith began to cut a square of red paper. Just then, the phone blared. Faith jumped, dropping the scissors. With a pounding heart, she lunged for the phone. "Yes?"

"This is the Towerton sheriff's office," the man on the other end said.

Faith was confused. They'd said they had to wait forty-eight hours to look for Winnie. The time wasn't up. "Have you found her?" Faith asked urgently.

"Pardon?"

"My friend, Winnie Gottlieb."

"No, ma'am. We're calling about an abandoned car which was left in an embankment. According to the registration it was rented to a Mr. Casper Reilly. Is he by any chance a guest at your place? We're checking all the local hotels and motels, since it was a rental."

"Yes! Yes, he's here," Faith told the man, hysteria rising in her voice. "Winnie Gottlieb was driving that car. I reported her missing last night."

"That car was pretty banged up, ma'am," said the officer. "She must have lost control and slid over the embankment. You're sure she was the driver?"

"Yes!" Faith cried impatiently. Why did he have to be so formal and slow? "She could be hurt. You have to find her. You can't wait any longer. She's been missing all night!"

"In this case we can begin a search," the officer said. "Can you please give me another description of Miss Gottlieb?"

Faith spoke rapidly in a breathless ramble, telling the officer anything that she thought might be helpful. "We'll begin right away," he assured her before he hung up.

Faith hung up quickly and began to cry. Heaving sobs wracked her. How had this happened? Why had she been so insensitive? The memory of her last conversation with Winnie haunted her. She'd been way too harsh. And then when Winnie had announced she was leaving, KC had tried to talk to her. Even Liza had made a last-ditch attempt to make her stay. But Faith hadn't. She'd simply gazed off at the falling snow as Winnie drove away—maybe forever.

At that moment, Faith became aware of a sound outside the front door. Someone was coming back. Had they found anything?

As the door swung open, Faith gasped. Winnie

stood before her looking just fine, rested, and healthy.

"Winnie!" Faith cried, leaping to her feet. "Oh, thank God!" She ran and wrapped Winnie in a tearful hug. "I've been so worried."

"And I thought you were still mad at me," said Winnie, clearly perplexed by this emotional greeting. She studied Faith's tear-stained face. "What's wrong? What happened?"

"We didn't know where you were. Everyone's out looking for you. Then the sheriff just called about the car and, well, I thought . . ." A new rush of tears overtook Faith.

"Gosh, I'm sorry everyone is in a panic," said Winnie.

"No. *I'm* sorry. I never should have yelled at you like I did. I'm really sorry," Faith apologized, thrilled to have this chance to speak to Winnie again. "Are you all right?"

"I am now. It's a long story. The bus was canceled and the car slid off the road. It could have been a real disaster, but look who was driving along and picked me up." Winnie gestured toward the jeep parked out front. All Faith could see was the back of a guy as he reached for something on the backseat. Then he turned around and waved to her.

Faith blinked in disbelief, but he was still there.

"I don't believe it!" she gasped, leaning against the door sill for support.

"Hi, beautiful!" Alec greeted her heartily, lugging his and Winnie's large bags up the steps. He stopped short when he saw that she'd been crying. "What's the matter?"

"Nothing now," Faith said, dazed. "I was so worried about Winnie."

Alec looked at Winnie with a raised eyebrow. "See? And you thought they didn't care."

"I just thought they'd figure I was already on a bus and on my way."

Suddenly the phone rang. "I'll get it," Winnie offered.

Curiously, Faith watched as she picked up the phone. "Hi, Mrs. Angeletti. Yes, I'm fine," Winnie spoke. "Sorry everyone was so worried. Yeah, what you heard in town is true. He's here. In fact, he's the one who saved me . . ."

Realizing everything was fine, Faith tuned out of the conversation and back to Alec. "I'm so glad to see you," she said sincerely. "This is a great surprise. I didn't think you'd come."

"I don't know how much private time we'll get," he told her. "Can you believe I've already been interviewed? For some reason Winnie wanted me to tell the whole world where I was staying. So I did."

"That was a super idea." Faith cried happily. "The ranch needs the publicity in a big way. Right now it would take a miracle to save it."

"A Christmas miracle, huh?"

"Yeah. And I think you're it." Slowly, the reality of the moment was all sinking in. Winnie was *really* safe. Alec Brady was *really, really* standing in front of her. Then Faith realized they were standing in the open doorway. "Hey, I'm sorry. Come on in." As she shut the door she caught a glimpse of her red, swollen face in the hall mirror. "God, I look a mess."

"You're a sight for sore eyes," Alec said warmly.

"So are you—the both of you," Faith said, her heart ready to burst with happiness. She stepped past him to go into the reception area, but he gently caught her arm. He pulled her back and kissed her hard on the lips.

Surprised, Faith staggered back a step. She smiled at him happily. "What was that for?"

With a twinkle in his eyes, Alec looked up to a green sprig someone had tacked over the doorway. "Mistletoe," he said. "Time to kiss again."

Twenty-three

ey, you guys! Cut that out!" Liza playfully scolded Casper and Kimberly. "No necking in the kitchen!"

The couple separated without completely breaking off their embrace. "Hi, Liza," said Casper.

Hands on her hips, Liza gazed at them. "I told you this was a budding romance. I saw it before either of you even knew it."

"That *is* true," Kimberly admitted. "How's the open house going?"

"Super," said Liza. "People are pouring in. I came in to put more appetizers in the oven."

"I've already got them heating up," Casper told her.

"Oh." Liza smirked. "I thought *you* two were the reason it was so hot in here."

"No, it's the oven," said Kimberly.

"Don't try to fool me," Liza said as she opened the oven door and sniffed the tiny quiches. "You've been grabbing each other since you came back from the Tower ranch the other night. It must have been quite a scene."

"It was," Kimberly smiled. "You should have seen Casper. He was like Clark Kent and Superman all at once."

"The avenging journalist, huh," said Liza. "You know what they say: The pen is mightier than the sword."

"I'm not so sure," Casper bantered, leaning against the counter. "Did I tell you I fenced?"

"You do?" cried Kimberly, impressed.

Liza looked at his slim figure, floppy hair, and glasses. Heroes came in all forms, she decided. "See, he's macho," Liza teased. "He's just living in the wrong century."

She pulled the tray of appetizers out of the oven. "I'd say these are done." Sliding them onto a serving platter, she headed for the door. "I'll leave you to your affairs, if you know what I mean."

"We'll be right out," said Kimberly.

"Yeah, sure," Liza replied, rolling her eyes. In the dining room people stood chatting, drinks in their hands. Mrs. Angeletti's impromptu Christmas Eve open house was turning into a huge success. Locals and tourists alike were coming to the event. All the merchants who had canceled two nights before were already there, even the ones who had complained about Winnie dumping dung in Suzanna's jeep. Liza guessed word was already out that Suzanna wasn't what she appeared. Jake Tower had probably seen to that.

And then there was the article in *The Towerton Gazette* that had appeared that very morning. Alec and Winnie were on the front page. And Alec was being great. He was making the rounds, talking to everyone.

"Isn't this the best?" said Faith, coming up alongside her. "The phone hasn't stopped ringing. The ranch is booked through most of January, too. Having Alec here was the answer all along."

"Can I have that in writing?" Liza asked.

Faith sighed without losing her happy expression. "Okay, well, you were right. But you should have told me to call him, not called him yourself."

"And what would you have said?" Liza challenged.

"No."

"So?"

"So, you did the right thing. In the wrong way . . . but it worked out, so who cares. You saved the ranch. You did. It's hard to believe, but indirectly, you did."

Liza beamed. Her daydream of being the heroine had come true. Having Faith admit it was the icing on the cake.

"Listen, Liza," Faith went on. "I want to say I'm sorry about Coyote. It was all my idea. At the time it just seemed funny. But I didn't mean for you to get hurt."

"I'm not hurt," Liza lied. She looked out into the crowded room and tried to imagine Coyote standing there. That's what it would have taken to make this day complete for her. But Coyote wasn't nowhere to be seen. "It was nice while it lasted," she said, trying to be philosophical.

"Those quiches are getting cold," Faith observed. "I'll serve them, if you'd like."

Liza handed her the tray. "Thanks. These will be gone in a second. I'll go into the kitchen and heat up more." As Faith made her rounds with the tray, Liza stood for a moment and surveyed the rapidly growing crowd.

Near the doorway Winnie stood with her arm around Josh, who had flown in from California that morning. Winnie had practically shone with happiness from the moment he arrived. Liza had almost forgotten how contagiously sunny Winnie could be when she was happy. After all that had happened, Winnie deserved to feel good.

Not far from her mother, KC circulated through the crowd, filling drinks and being her most gracious. She looked more beautiful than ever in a flowing, rose-print dress, her dark hair gathered into a loose knot. Like Winnie, KC also seemed transformed by love. The hardness Liza so disliked in KC had melted. In its place was something intangible but real. A softness. Liza liked this new KC.

Which leaves me, the same as always, the eternal single, she thought regretfully. *Typical. My one big romance turns out to be a big mistake.* "Oh, well," she muttered as she turned to go into the kitchen. Everybody couldn't be starry-eyed. Somebody had to heat up the appetizers.

Then, from the corner of her eye, she spotted a familiar face standing in the doorway. It was Coyote, dressed in a western-style blue suit with a bolo tie. He held his cowboy hat in his hand as he craned his neck in search of someone. Was he looking for her?

His eyes lit as he spotted her. Liza stood frozen to her spot while he made his way across the room. What did he want? Did he have some last cutting words to deliver?

"Merry Christmas," he said quietly when he reached her.

"It's only Christmas Eve," Liza snapped.

Coyote smiled. "I heard you were having this open house, and I figured I owed you something."

"You don't owe me anything."

"Yes, I do," he insisted. "I promised you a free performance. The guys are all with me, ready to play."

Liza stepped back in surprise. "That would be terrific." Despite her pride, she knew it would be just the thing to make this party unforgettable. For Mrs. Angeletti's sake she couldn't say no. She didn't want to say no, anyway. She wanted to keep him here. "I guess you should set up in here, but I'll go ask Mrs. A. Maybe she wants to use the Lazy Q room."

Liza started to walk toward Mrs. Angeletti, but Coyote took hold of her wrist. "Liza, I'm sorry if I said mean things the other night. I was embarrassed at being tricked. But then I got to thinking about the snowlady we built together. I like you a lot."

"I like you, too," Liza admitted quietly. "And I don't think you were tricked. They might not have known it, but Faith and Kimberly were telling the truth. I liked you right from the start."

"So did I."

Coyote held out his arms and pulled her to him. Liza's heart was soaring. "Now, cowboy," she said, smiling up at him, "let's get this party rollin'."

"Oh—eee!" he cried. "Yes, ma'am!"

Later that night, KC sat out at the reception desk and watched the lights of the Christmas tree sparkle. It was hard to believe that everything had turned out so well.

"What are you doing out here?" Winnie asked, running in from the dining room. "Everybody is doing one of those group-dance things. You know, where you stamp and clap and shuffle around all together. It's fun."

"Thanks, but I'll stay here," KC declined. "I'm kind of tired. So much has happened and I'm a little beat."

"Are you thinking about Jeremy?" Winnie asked.

"I guess so. I can't stop thinking about him in the hospital on Christmas Eve. I'd have liked to go visit him, but I couldn't leave Mom today."

"The important thing is that he's going to be all right," said Winnie. "He has you to thank for that, too. I can't believe you ran out into that arena to help him. That was so brave."

"I wasn't thinking, I was just moving."

"It was still brave," said Winnie, heading back toward the dining room.

"Win," KC called after her. "Is everything okay now? I mean, between us?"

Winnie smiled at her. "Sure," she said. "But if you ever yell at me again, I'm going to put you in my pocketbook."

"What?" KC questioned, knitting her brow.

"Nothing," said Winnie. "We'll always be friends, KC. No matter what."

"No matter what," KC echoed with a smile. "Thanks for everything you've done around here."

"You're welcome," Winnie said. Then she turned and hurried back into the dining room.

KC listened to the music. The band was playing a lively country song. Everyone jumping, clapping, and turning at once sounded like thunder. The Lonely Rangers had turned the party from merely pleasant into a real bash.

"There you are," said her mother, coming out to find her. "Are you feeling all right?"

"I'm fine, Mom. I just needed a break." As she spoke, another guest came through the front door. And then another hobbled through on one crutch.

KC leapt to her feet. It was old Mr. Tower, dressed in a stetson and a long gray topcoat. He held the door open for Jeremy, who smiled brightly at her as he took off his cowboy hat.

"Welcome," said Mrs. Angeletti, sounding a little nervous.

"I hope you'll forgive us crashing your party," said Mr. Tower. "But I believe turnabout is fair play."

"Absolutely," Mrs. Angeletti agreed. "One party-crashing deserves another."

"Why are you out of the hospital?" KC asked rushing to Jeremy's side.

"It's Christmas," he said with a smile. "Remember?"

KC put her hand tenderly on his shoulder. "I remember. And I'm so happy to see you," she murmured gently.

"I couldn't stay away." Jeremy gazed into her eyes. "You look like an angel."

"My dear woman," Mr. Tower said to Mrs. Angeletti. "There is a lot we have to discuss. I have mistakenly caused you many problems, for which I apologize. And, thanks to your daughter, I may now have a chance to save my ranch. I owe her a debt I can never repay."

"I was only trying to help my mother," said KC, keeping her hand on Jeremy's shoulder.

"Well, in the process you have helped me, and more than that, you have given me back my grandson."

"That makes me happy," said KC. "Merry Christmas."

"Merry Christmas to you," Mr. Tower replied. "From now on we will be true neighbors. Jeremy and I have been discussing ways in which to save our ranches. And as for Ms. Cartlyn, I'm having her investigated for embezzlement. I don't think we'll have any more trouble from her."

"I'm so glad," said Mrs. Angeletti. "Come inside and have something to eat and drink. There'll be plenty of time to talk after Christmas."

Taking his arm, Mrs. Angeletti drew Mr. Tower into the dining room. "Is there someplace we can be alone?" Jeremy asked KC. "I mean really alone."

KC nodded. "We can go outside."

Taking her jacket from the closet, she led the way to the terrace. A fat full moon hung in the sky above the white mountains. "How beautiful," she said.

"Not nearly as beautiful as you," Jeremy told her. "I don't know how you came into my life, Kahia Cayanne. But I'm glad I recognized you as someone special when I saw you."

"I recognized you, too," said KC.

Jeremy smiled lovingly and gathered her under his good arm. They stood a moment gazing up at the moon. "It's funny," he said. "It's freezing cold, but I'm warm."

"So am I." KC reached up and kissed his lips.

He kissed her back, squeezing her even closer.

"From the very beginning I knew you would change my life," he whispered when they broke apart. "But I had no idea how much. You've saved it in more ways than you can imagine."

KC gazed up into his dark handsome eyes, and she understood something beyond a doubt. Jeremy hadn't pulled her away from a bull, but he had saved her life, just the same. He had unearthed a core in her, a spirit, that was slowly unfurling its wings.

Holding each other tight under the Christmas moon, KC knew in her heart that no matter what lay ahead for them, there was no going back.

America's hottest new television series . . .

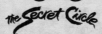

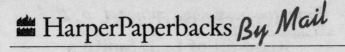